MIDSUMMER PASSION

& OTHER TALES OF MAINE CUSSEDNESS

ERSKINE

MIDSU
PASS

CALDWELL

MMER
ON

& OTHER TALES OF MAINE CUSSEDNESS

INTRODUCTION BY UPTON BIRNIE BRADY

EDITED BY CHARLES G. WAUGH AND MARTIN H. GREENBERG

YANKEE BOOKS
CAMDEN · MAINE

Reprinted by permission of McIntosh and Otis, Inc.
for the estate of Erskine Caldwell

PRIMING THE WELL
© 1931 Erskine Caldwell
A WOMAN IN THE HOUSE
© 1933 Erskine Caldwell
THE AUTOMOBILE THAT
WOULDN'T RUN
© 1930 Erskine Caldwell
BALM OF GILEAD
© 1939 Erskine Caldwell
AN AUTUMN COURTSHIP
© 1931 Erskine Caldwell
THE WINDFALL
© 1942 Erskine Caldwell
A VERY LATE SPRING
© 1930 Erskine Caldwell
TEN THOUSAND
BLUEBERRY CRATES
© 1931 Erskine Caldwell
THE SICK HORSE
© 1934 Erskine Caldwell
THE CORDUROY PANTS
© 1931 Erskine Caldwell

THE RUMOR
© 1931 Erskine Caldwell
OVER THE GREEN
MOUNTAINS
© 1935 Erskine Caldwell
COUNTRY FULL OF SWEDES
© 1932 Erskine Caldwell
THE DREAM
© 1931 Erskine Caldwell
THE MIDWINTER GUEST
© 1932 Erskine Caldwell
THE MATING OF MARJORIE
© 1930 Erskine Caldwell
THE LONELY DAY
© 1931 Erskine Caldwell
JOHN THE INDIAN AND
GEORGE HOPKINS
© 1930 Erskine Caldwell
THE GRASS FIRE
© 1935 Erskine Caldwell
MIDSUMMER PASSION
© 1929 Erskine Caldwell

COVER AND TEXT DESIGN BY LURELLE CHEVERIE

Typeset by Camden Type 'n Graphics, Camden, Maine
Printed and bound by BookCrafters, Chelsea, Michigan

Library of Congress Cataloging-in-Publication Data

Caldwell, Erskine, 1903–
    Midsummmer passion & other tales of Maine cussedness / Erskine Caldwell :
introduction by Upton Birnie Brady : edited by Charles C. Waugh and Martin
Harry Greenberg.
        p.   cm.
    ISBN 0-89909-214-4
    1. Maine–Fiction. I. Waugh, Charles. II. Greenberg, Martin Harry. III. Title.
PS3505.A322M53   1990
813'.52–dc20   90-12530
                                                                    CIP

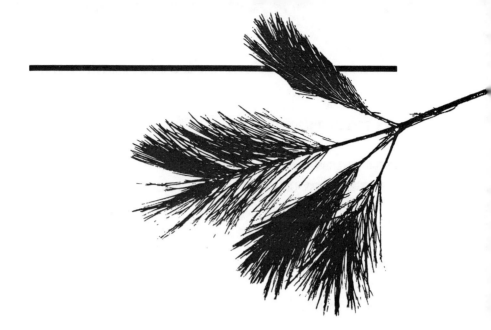

CONTENTS

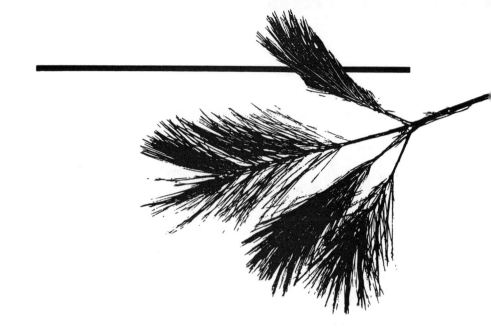

INTRODUCTION

When the publisher of Yankee Books first showed me this collection of stories by Erskine Caldwell, I was a bit incredulous. Erskine Caldwell writing stories about Maine? I was even more surprised to learn Caldwell's first published story was about Maine.

If we think of him at all, we New Englanders tend to think of Erskine Caldwell as a "Southern writer,"—one of those odd folk from below the Mason-Dixon line. We think of people with names like Jeeter Lester and Darling Jill Walden, we think of rural Southern poverty and squalid sex, "huggin' and rubbin' " in the tobacco field, and of course we think of "banned in Boston." In 1955, Stanley Kunitz wrote in *Twentieth Century Authors* that "Caldwell's phenomenal success has continued in spite of (and possibly because of) the fact that his works have been subjected to more censorship than those of any other American author." By 1970, his publishers estimated that his books had sold sixty million copies worldwide. Obviously, one concludes, it was because of their salacious content. (Faulkner, who included Caldwell in a very small handful of American writers whose work he considered first class, nevertheless noted that his work "grew towards trash.")

Though censorship no doubt helped Erskine Caldwell in the sense that notoriety sells books, it obscured the real value of his work. If you reread *Tobacco Road* or Caldwell's masterpiece, *God's Little Acre*, as I have just done, you will find that by today's standards (in comparison, say, with Carolyn Chute's *The Beans of Egypt, Maine*, or even with Judy Blume's novels intended for teenagers), Caldwell's writing is tame, indeed. What used to be considered too rough for the genteel tastes of the literati now can be seen for what it really is, a genuine appreciation of the vitality of the human spirit under the most trying circumstances of poverty, depression, and neglect, a celebration of the pure cussedness of people who refuse to be put down.

The incredulity I first felt on hearing of these Maine stories quickly changed to delight as I read them. They seemed quite unlike anything I expected. Rather than the grinding poverty of Southern stories, here we find only the tight-fistedness for which the denizens of Maine are famous. There is no hint that the writer is actually a Southerner, and little, if any sex, either overt or of the flaring-nostrils and heaving-breasts sort that is usually referred to as "soft-core." What I did find were characters that were immediately recognizable as real people—crusty people—and as people from New England. And in the form and style of the stories, I found not the old-fashioned *Saturday Evening Post* sort of thing that one expects of stories written in the 1930s and '40s, with predictable situations and easy, artificial resolutions, but rather stories that were as up-to-date as anything written last year. If I were forced to categorize these stories (and there is no reason why I should, since such categorizations are for the use of academics seeking tenure, not to enhance the enjoyment of readers), I might be tempted to call them "minimalist" or even "post-modern," (whatever that means).

But labels, no matter how fancy, fail to do justice to the continued vitality and immediacy of these stories. The simple fact is that with the passage of time and the settling of the dust raised by censors, Erskine Caldwell has emerged as a writer for all time, whose success depends not on the region about which he is writing, but on his acute

INTRODUCTION

perception of the foibles of human nature, whether in the South or the North. It is a great pleasure, then, to find that Erskine Caldwell, a quintessentially Southern writer, has written so much and so well about New England. But how did Caldwell come to write these stories?

Erskine Caldwell was born in White Oak, Georgia, on December 17, 1903. His father was a minister of the Associate Reformed Presbyterian Church who moved about from parish to parish, mainly in Georgia and the Carolinas, in search of a livelihood. Far from dislocating young Caldwell (though, by his own account in his autobiography *With All My Might*, he suffered briefly each time they moved), this itinerant life apparently gave Caldwell a zest for change and variety that he never lost. Tutored at home by his mother, he lived a life free of the usual constraints of school, which seems to have nurtured not only the imagination of a writer but an enterprising spirit as well. In each new town, Caldwell managed to find some small job to earn pocket money. Among other things, he delivered shoes, sorted mail and sold laundry bluing and subscriptions to "Grit," the weekly magazine for boys.

In the summer of 1917, just after the U.S. had entered World War I, Caldwell, then fourteen years old, took a job as a driver at the Millington Army Base, near Memphis. The job only lasted for the summer, but it was his first experience of living away from home for any length of time, and he wrote up his adventures in a brief novel entitled *A Boy's Own Story of City Life*, which he duly showed his parents. So shocked were they, not by the contents of the book, but by his woeful lack of expertise in spelling, punctuation, and handwriting, that he was immediately enrolled in the local public school. Paradoxically, this early discouragement only convinced him more strongly that he wanted to be a writer.

Two years later he took the first step toward becoming a professional writer when he was employed, without pay, as printer's devil for the *Jefferson Reporter*, a small weekly in Wrens, Georgia, where his family had recently moved. After he had been on the job a few months, the editor of the paper went on a lengthy fishing trip, leaving Caldwell in charge. He wrote all the copy, set it into type, printed it, and delivered 600 copies to the post office for distribution to subscribers. The only things he did not do were sell advertisements and collect money for the subscriptions. This prompted him to ask for a salary, a request that the editor found insupportable. But Caldwell's confidence in his reporting ability was confirmed, and it wasn't long before he was employed as a stringer for the Augusta *Chronicle,* reporting local sporting events.

Caldwell never graduated from high school: He had not accumulated enough credits. But the principal kindly agreed to allow him to accept a blank scroll on graduation day, when the other twenty-six members of his class would receive their diplomas. "Even more than being stoical in such a situation," Caldwell writes, "I felt that I had achieved a measure of superior experience and practical knowledge for use in the future that could not have been gained in a dutiful adherence to scholarly studies alone."

Somehow, his father arranged for Erskine a scholarship to his old alma mater, Erskine College, an institution run by the Associate Reform Presbyterian Church. He soon wearied of the religious tone of the place, however, and in the spring of his second year he simply left—we would nowadays call it "dropping out." He kicked around the South a while, ending in jail in Bogalusa, Louisiana, as a vagrant. It took a letter to his father, smuggled out of jail, to free him. On his return home, his father's only comment was: "What did you think of Louisiana, son? It's a much different part of the world, isn't it?"

"Unpromising as the future may have been in the spring of the year 1922," Caldwell wrote, "nevertheless I was in no mood to allow myself to be discouraged. I remained determined to find a way to become a student at the University of Virginia.

"Diligently combing and scanning and rereading all the university materials I could obtain, I was elated to discover late one night in the month of May that I might be able to qualify for and perhaps be granted a tuition-paid scholarship.... It was offered neither on the basis of merit or need. And the grant provided the full amount of tuition for a period of four years." The scholarship Caldwell had lit upon required nothing, academic or otherwise, other than that the recipient be a direct descendant of a soldier in the Confederate Army during the Civil War.

After two years in Charlottesville, "having associated with students from many regions of the United States, I was well aware that I would never be content until I could put myself beyond the confines of the South so that my vision of life would be that of an American and not solely that of a Southerner. Resolutely, and with no thought of what hazards might be in store for me, I went to Philadelphia on the train and entered the summer session of the Wharton School at the University of Pennsylvania for the study of advanced economics." He supported himself that summer as a night counterman in a fast-food

INTRODUCTION

joint. On finishing the term, he took a job at Kresge's in Wilkes-Barre to put his new-found economic knowledge to the test of practical merchandising. But by the next term—the spring term of 1925—he was back at the University of Virginia, and before the end of the term he had fallen in love and married Helen Lannigan, an attractive blonde graduate student whom he had literally bumped into on his way out of one of his classes.

Suddenly faced with the responsibilities of marriage, Caldwell soon found a job as a reporter on the Atlanta *Journal,* and moonlighted as a book reviewer for the Charlotte *Observer* and, later, the Houston *Post*. But twenty-five dollars a week was not enough, even when supplemented by the sale of innumerable review copies of books, at a quarter apiece, to used-book dealers. He determined to find a way to live cheaply until he could become established as a writer, as well as to satisfy his continuing urge to see some part of the United States besides the South. In 1926, he and Helen moved to a three-story, ten-room, unheated, eighteenth-century house in Mount Vernon, Maine, his parents-in-law's summer house.

"One of the principal reasons," Caldwell writes, "for favoring the state of Maine as a suitable place to live for several years was that I felt the need to go as far away as possible in order to gain a revealing perspective of the scenes and circumstances of life in the South. . . .

"Another reason, and it was an important one, for the decision to leave Georgia for Maine was the offer to become caretaker of the farm and buildings in Mount Vernon where, for our own use, I would be able to grow potatoes and rutabagas for food and to cut wood for warmth. At the time, being able to live free of rent and grow our own food was a highly opportune event in our lives when our only source of income was from the sale of a review copy of a book for twenty-five cents."

With his usual forthright attitude toward any obstacle that stood in his way, Caldwell set immediately to work planting crops and cutting wood. The first summer he cut ten cords of green birch. His neighbor, Arthur Doloff, when called upon to admire this achievement, only remarked, "Cussed birch won't make heat when it's green and won't do nothing but make ashes when it's dry."

And he wrote. Although the temperature fell well below zero most winter nights, and his workroom upstairs was completely unheated, Caldwell wrapped himself in layers of clothing and blankets as he typed away. He and Helen lived mainly on rutabagas and potatoes in the winter, with apples for dessert occasionally, and sold review copies of books (of which he had accumulated some three thousand at this point) when they needed cash. By 1928, they had two sons as well as themselves to feed. And it was in that year that his first published story appeared. It was "Midsummer Passion," printed in *transition*, an English-language magazine published in Paris. He had recently sold a parcel of review books, and with the few dollars remaining from the sale he and Helen celebrated by taking the boys to the village store and gorging themselves on walnut-fudge ice cream.

But within the next five years, Erskine Caldwell's career was made. His first novel, *The Bastard*, was published in 1929. In 1930, Maxwell Perkins of Charles Scribner's Sons published *American Earth*. *Tobacco Road* followed in 1932 and *God's Little Acre*, generally held to be Caldwell's masterpiece, in 1933. In the same year, he won an award from the *Yale Review* for his story "Country Full of Swedes." The censors, including Boston's own Watch and Ward Society, did their best to prevent *Tobacco Road* from being sold, and the play based on it (which ran for seven and a half years on Broadway—a record at the time) from being seen, but that, of course, only increased Caldwell's fame and spurred the sales of his books.

By 1938, Caldwell's marriage to Helen had fallen apart, and he moved from Maine to Connecticut. He still had a long and active career ahead of him—forty novels, two children's books, four collections of stories, four text-and-picture books with Margaret Bourke-White (his second wife) and two books with his fourth wife, Virginia Caldwell, as well as many screenplays. But, though some of the later work is very good, it does not as a whole hold up to the consistent vigor and liveliness of the books and stories he produced while living in Mount Vernon. By 1943, though Caldwell seemed to have all he could want out of life, he nevertheless felt "yearnings for a quiet retreat as comforting and productive as it had been my good fortune to enjoy in Mount Vernon for many years." And throughout the rest of his life, though he had his choice of where he might live, and moved often, and travelled all over the world, he always felt a certain nostalgia for those hard but amazingly productive years he spent in Maine.

Was it the air? The brilliantly cloudless summer days of hot sun and cool breeze? Perhaps even the frost-bound winters, or the exercise necessary to cultivate hundreds of pounds of potatoes and rutabagas and to cut and split dozens of cords of wood? I will leave it to a biographer to decide just what it was that Maine did for Erskine Caldwell. Whatever it was, readers of these stories will see that they have very good reasons to be grateful for it.

INTRODUCTION

And what of these stories? They are all set in Maine, and they all have to do, one way or another, as the subtitle of this book claims, with cussedness. What is cussedness? It is, of course, as Arthur Doloff pointed out, what makes birch firewood give no heat when it is green and nothing but ash when it is seasoned. It is not restricted to New England, but it tends to be possessed in fuller measure by "dam-yankees," like the wife in "Priming the Well" who knows just how to sell a farm for top dollar during a drought. It's what irritates Max Clough about having "A Woman in the House." It's what makes Mal Anderson push his car to court his girlfriend Signe after someone has stolen the motor from it. It is nothing but cussedness that makes Ned Jones argue with a New Hampshire insurance company about the exact value of lightning rods, and take surprising remedial action when they disagree with him. Cussedness causes poor Amos Williams to take the wrong tack when trying to marry Esther for her quilts, since his sister got married the previous spring and left him with only a few thin blankets.

In "The Windfall," Caldwell gives us a glance at another aspect of cussedness: "From Bangor to Burlington, all the Murdocks, especially the home-owning branch of the family, were known throughout the entire region north of Boston for their trait, which relatives and other outsiders called cussedness, of not acknowledging kinship with one another." Without a fair dose of cussedness, Mary Jane would not know how to cope with the effect of "A Very Late Spring" nor Walt Brown with the taunts of Nate Emmonds. And wasn't it pure cussedness that gripped Benton when he swapped his perfectly good horse Jim Dandy for King, an ailing nag, plus a rusty mowing machine?

Cussedness runs through these stories like a musical motif, and I will leave the reader to spot it in the stories included in this delightful volume that I have not mentioned here. It is a characteristic that Erskine Caldwell admired in all human beings, but found in abundance in the people of Maine, and I believe that until he saw it so lavishly at work in the environs of Mount Vernon, he could not get a grip on how it manifested itself in the people of the South with whom he was so much more familiar. Dessie's anxious digging behind the barn in "The Windfall" is, I am convinced, a forerunner of Ty Ty Walden's endless, almost mythic search for gold on his property in *God's Little Acre*. And finally, in the neighborly tussle of "Midsummer Passion" an astute reader will be able to see a hint of Caldwell's attitude toward relations between the sexes, an attitude so far from the categories of "obscene" or "prurient" to which the censors assigned them that nowadays we can only laugh at the poor benighted censors, while celebrating the wry humor and poignancy of these stories.

Erskine Caldwell's short stories are not as famous—or as notorious—as his novels *Tobacco Road* or *God's Little Acre*, and they comprise only a small fraction of his immense *oeuvre*. Of these, the Maine stories are an even smaller fraction. And yet they are as good as anything he wrote. They show a picture of the country and the people he is writing about that is instantly recognizable as *true*, a picture powered not by literary gimmicks or "fine writing," but by the good, old-fashioned, indomitable cussedness of human beings.

UPTON BIRNIE BRADY
Bedford, Massachusetts
May 1, 1990

PRIMING THE
WELL

When I was a little fellow my mother, who was half damyankee, used to tell me the story about wooden nutmegs. Even now I can clearly remember her picturing the early peddlers with pouches of painted nutmegs going from farm to farm along the Potomac, selling the spice with all the solemnity of a Methodist circuit-rider. That the nutmegs were easily sold and eagerly bought is beside the story; the wonder is that we Southerners were so dumb we did not know the difference.

For some reason I never fully understood, my mother and father, when I was still quite young, went Down East as far as they could and bought a farm in the Kennebec River Valley. Then, when I was eleven years old and my sister nine, they decided that they would sell the farm and move back to Virginia. This was the easiest phase of the decision, because finding somebody who wanted to invest six thousand dollars in a Maine farm was a problem difficult to solve. Even when we did find a purchaser it was by mere accident that the sale was so easily made.

It was a three-months' drought that finally brought a buyer to us. And that was chance, too; because droughts for more than three or four weeks were uncommon where we were.

Since I have grown older I have come to the conclusion that my father was by inheritance a New Englander himself, or else he had never got over the brooding humiliation of his descent from buyers of wooden nutmegs. And then too, of course, my mother was half damyankee.

In the late spring, about four months before the drought came to an end,—the last rain fell on the first day of June— there were two men who were very anxious to buy our farm. The price either of them was willing to pay at that time, however, was not much more than one half the figure my father had placed on it. Mr. Geroux, a Frenchman, was one of the prospective purchasers, and Elisha Goodwin the other. Mr. Geroux was a native of New Brunswick, but he had lived in Maine thirty years or longer. He had become unusually prosperous in recent years because of the rising market for seed potatoes, and during all that time he had been unconsciously acquiring that same cautious mind Elisha Goodwin had inherited from six generations of forefathers. Both of these men, however, realized the value of our farm and both knew it was worth every dollar of six thousand. Neither of them was willing, though, to pay the price asked until he was sure it could not be bought for less. And, as we were told afterwards, Mr. Geroux would have paid almost anything up to ten thousand for the farm, because its improvements, fertility, and location were making it increasingly valuable.

PRIMING THE WELL

In the month of August, the beginning of the last month of the terrible drought, both Mr. Geroux and Elisha Goodwin came to see my father in regard to purchasing our farm. They did not come together, of course, because each of them wanted to buy it before the other did. At the same time, each of them wanted to close the deal before he was forced to bid against the other. The month of August was the dryest ever to be recorded in the State of Maine. Everyone was certain of that. No rain had fallen since the first of June. The Kennebec River was so low that it was out of the question for the paper-mills to float pulpwood, and all of those which were not importing Scandinavian baled pulp had to close down. Even the lakes in the back-country were so low that at least fifty per cent of the fish had already died. There was nothing that could be done about the weather, though, and everybody just had to wait for fall to come, bringing rain or snow. Towards the end of the month the water famine was becoming dangerous. The farmers, whose wells had gone dry and who had been drawing water from the river and lakes, were faced with additional danger when the river went completely dry along with most of the lakes. The stock on every farm was dropping dead day and night. There had been no milk in the valley for nearly a month, and the horses, steers, and sheep were hungry and thirsty. The month of August was without exception the most damaging month in the history of the entire Kennebec River Valley.

There was a deep lake on our farm about a mile and a half from the buildings and we were fortunate in having some water for our stock and ourselves. We drew water to the house every day from the lake. Our well had gone dry just as quickly as all the other wells in the valley.

We had been drawing water in three barrels every day from the lake. After six weeks of this my father became tired of having to go to the lake every day. He decided that we would draw twenty-five or thirty barrels one day a week and store it on the farm. This would save us the trouble of having to go every day and give us time to do some other work that was needed. The real problem, however, was where and how to store a week's supply of water. It would have been foolish to buy twenty-five or thirty barrels, or even half that many, when we could use them at the most only two or three weeks longer. Then they would have to be stored away and they would dry and warp until they were valueless. I believe it was my mother who made the suggestion of storing the water in the well. At least, it was she who said it was the only place she knew about. At first my father was of the opinion that the water would run or seep out of the well faster than we could haul it, but he was willing to try it, anyway. The plan worked, much to my mother's joy. All of us—my father, my sister, and myself—congratulated her on making such a wise suggestion.

We went to work at once and all that day we drew water from the lake and poured it into the well. By late afternoon we had transferred about thirty or thirty-five barrels of lake water to the well. That evening all we had to do was to lower the bucket and bring up as much water as we needed for the stock. The next day it was the same. The water was still there and apparently none had seeped away. It was a great improvement over the way we had been doing before.

It was by accident that Elisha Goodwin stopped at our house that afternoon. His horse had thrown a shoe and he came up to the barn to draw out the nails so the hoof would not be injured. He came up to the barn where we were at the time.

"Well, Mr. Langley," he said to my father, "what are we going to do about this here drought? The whole State of Maine will be ruined if this keeps up another two weeks. There ain't a drop of water on my whole farm."

"The drought is terrible," my father said. "I won't have even a peck of potatoes out of the whole farm to sell this year. But, strange to say, I've got plenty of water in my well."

"What?" Mr. Goodwin shouted unbelievingly. "You say you got water in your well?"

"Plenty of it."

"Well, I don't believe it. Nobody else has got any water in their wells. How comes it you got water in your'n?"

"I water my stock from it twice a day and we have plenty of water for the kitchen besides. It's just as full as it's ever been."

Elisha Goodwin thought we were joking with him about having plenty of water in the well, but he went over to see for himself just the same.

My father sent my sister into the house.

Elisha Goodwin picked up three or four pebbles and leaned far over the well looking down into it and trying to see the water. He dropped one of the pebbles into the well and cocked his head sideways, listening for the *ker-plunk* the stone made when it struck the water. He repeated this as long as his pebbles lasted. Then he stood up and looked at us. By watching his face we could tell that he was getting ready to say something important.

He stood up looking at us and scratching the top of his head with three of his fingers while his hatbrim was held tightly by the other two. His chin-whiskers moved up and down faster than I could count.

"How much is it you're asking for this place of your'n?"

My father told him how much we were holding it for.

"You haven't closed a deal with anybody yet, have you?"

"Well, not exactly," my father stated. "Though Mr. Geroux has asked me to give him a two-months' option on the place."

"Did you let him have it?" Elisha Goodwin asked hurriedly.

"I'm to let him know to-morrow about it," my father said.

"You come with me to the village," Elisha Goodwin said. "We'll fix up a sale before sundown. I'm going to buy your place. It's the only farm in the whole gol-darned State that's got any well-water on it."

"Are you sure you want to buy it, Mr. Goodwin?" my father asked him. "You know the price and terms. It's six thousand dollars cash."

"I don't give a gol-darn what your terms are. I'm going to pay you six thousand dollars in cash for it as soon as you go to the village with me and draw up a bill of sale and turn over the deed. I ain't going to let that good-for-nothing Canuck get his hands on the best farm in the whole gol-darned country. Come on to the village and get it settled right away."

Instead of driving to the village in the buggy, he and my father went in our automobile. He left his horse and buggy hitched at our barn. They were gone about two hours.

When they came back they shook hands with each other and Elisha Goodwin drove home at a fast clip. He must have forgotten about his horse throwing a shoe.

My mother came out with my sister and asked us what agreement had been made. My father told her all about it. She smiled a little but did not say anything just then. While I carried water to the stock and while my sister went down into the cellar to get some potatoes for supper, they walked across the pasture talking to themselves about something they did not want us to overhear. When they came back we all went into the kitchen while supper was cooking.

"Well, we are moving back to Virginia next week," my father told us, smiling at my mother. "As soon as we can pack everything we want to take with us we're leaving."

He called my sister to him and lifted her on his knee. He stroked her curls absent-mindedly several times.

"Louise," he smiled at her, "tell me: are you a little Virginia girl, or are you a little New Englander?"

My sister answered without a moment's hesitation.

"I'd rather be a little Virginia lady."

"But your mother is a damyankee—don't you want to be like her?"

He always smiled to himself when he called my mother a damyankee. I had looked for the word in the dictionary we had, but I could never find it anywhere.

Before my sister could reply, my mother came over where we were and lifted her to the floor from my father's lap.

"Louise, you and Tommy run out into the yard and play until supper is ready. Run along, now."

We left the kitchen and went out on the porch. Hardly before we were down the front steps, we heard two people laughing as though they had just seen the funniest thing in the world. We tiptoed to the kitchen window and looked in to see what was so funny. Both my mother and father were standing in the middle of the kitchen floor holding on to each other and laughing so hard I thought they would burst open if they kept it up much longer.

My sister pulled me by the arm and pointed down the river. The sky down there was the blackest I have ever seen. The black clouds were coming closer and closer all the time, like somebody covering you with a big black blanket at night. Away down the valley we could see the tops of the trees bending over so far that many of them broke off and fell to the ground.

"Look!" my sister said, clutching my arm. She was trembling all over. "Look!"

Holding each other tightly by the hand, we ran into the house as fast as we could so that the storm would not get us.

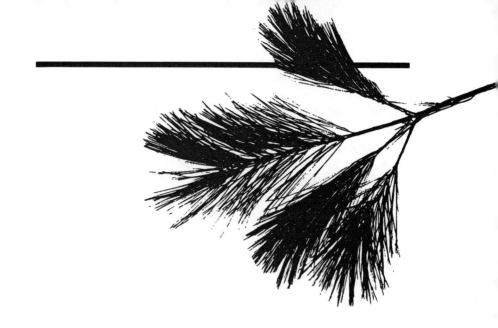

A WOMAN
IN THE HOUSE

Max Clough was getting along well enough until
Elam went away over the week-end. Max had
his winter's wood in, his house was sawdust-
banked against the frost, and there was a good
supply of pumpkin wine in the cellar. He had
settled himself for a good three months' rest and
he thought Elam had done the same. Both of
them knew that winter was coming, as the
ground was frozen every morning, and the sun
was already beginning to set in the intervale by
two o'clock.

But Elam went away over the week-end. He
went off without coming to tell Max about it, and

he left early Saturday morning before it was light enough for Max to see him go.

Only a few days before, Max had gone across the road and talked for an hour or longer, but Elam had not said a word about going away. He had not even said that he was thinking of taking a short trip. They had talked about how dear money was getting to be, and how much improved the mail delivery was since Cliff Stone had taken over the route through the intervale, and about the prospects for a new State highroad through the town. But Elam had said nothing about his going away over the week-end. That was the reason why Max was upset Saturday morning when he went across the road to see Elam a moment, and found that the house was locked and that the shades were drawn.

"When a man gets to be thirty-six years old," Max said, looking sharply at the closed dwelling, "he ought to have sense enough to stay at home, instead of going off for week-ends in Lewiston and throwing away dear money for lodging and what-not. Elam might possess a little sense about minor things, but he hasn't got the sense he was born with when it comes to throwing away dear money in Lewiston. Nobody but a plain fool would go to Lewiston and give a woman five-ten dollars for her bed."

He went back across the road and up the slope to his own house, glancing up the intervale and down it, as if he expected to see Elam coming home. But he knew Elam would not come home until Sunday afternoon. He had gone away before like that, and each time he had stayed the two whole days. He knew Elam would not return until the next afternoon.

Max's farm and buildings were on the eastern slope of the intervale, and Elam Stairs' were on the western slope. Between them was the Yorkfield town road. The only advantage Elam had, Max admitted, was longer sunlight in winter. The sun set on Max's house by two o'clock in midwinter, while Elam had an hour's longer sun. But Max was well enough pleased with his place, because he knew that his eastern slope grew better green peas. His land was well watered the year around; in midsummer, Elam's fields became dry.

For the rest of the afternoon and far into the evening, Max could not get off his mind Elam's trip. He did not envy him the week end in Lewiston, because he knew exactly how much it would cost, but he did not wish for Elam to slip off as he did three or four times a year. It upset his carefully planned living. He could do nothing while Elam was absent from home. He had become accustomed to seeing Elam somewhere about his farm at almost any hour of the day when he looked over at the western slope, and when Elam was not there, Max was at a loss to know how to continue doing his work. And, besides that, when Elam was away, there was always the possibility that he would not come back alone. He knew he could never get over Elam's bringing home somebody with him.

They had talked such things over many times. Each time Elam went to Lewiston, he came home talking about the women he had seen on the streets and in the lodginghouses. That was one reason why Max did not like for Elam to go there. Sooner or later, he knew Elam would bring home a woman.

"The women aren't suited to our lives, Elam," Max told him once. "You on your western slope, and me on my eastern slope, live as people ought to live. Just as soon as a man brings home a woman, his house is too small a space for him to live in, eight rooms or twelve rooms. Married, or housekeeper, there's no difference. It's a woman, and there's always trouble under a roof when you mix the two sexes. I wish to stay just as I am. I wish to live peacefully, and my wish is to die the same way."

"Can't somehow always agree with you, Max," Elam said, shaking his head. "You've got a lot of sense; good, sane, horse sense, Max. But God was required to make woman. Why! do you know that before there were any women, the men were fixing to tear the world to pieces unless women were provided?"

"Why?" Max asked.

"Why?" Elam said. "Why! because the men wouldn't stand for it any longer, that's why. They had to have housekeepers, or if they couldn't be had, just wives. There's a world of difference between the two, but at bottom they both are women, and that's what man had to have. Otherwise, us men would have to do all the sewing and cooking."

"Have always got along fairly well doing my own labor," Max said. "Never had a woman to do my work for me. I don't wish to have one in the house to cause trouble."

"Well," Elam said, "they may cause some trouble. I'm willing to grant you that. But taking all in all, their good points pretty well overbalance the bad ones. God was compelled to make them, and I don't aim to disuse anything that is provided. Guess I wish to get all there is in this life to make use of. No sense in letting it go to waste, or to have somebody else take my share, and his too. I wish to have all of everything that's due me."

Max was not convinced then, and he was still firm in his belief that a man could live more happily and peacefully in his house alone. None of the times when Elam tried to make Max admit that women were a necessary part of existence did he succeed. Max was steadfast in his determination to live his life apart from women.

Now that Elam had gone away on another of his quarterly trips to Lewiston, Max was afraid once again that he would bring home a housekeeper. On each occasion before, he had been on edge the whole time Elam was away, and he was never able to calm himself until he could go over and see that Elam had not brought back a housekeeper. He would not even take Elam's word for it. He would first ask Elam if he came home alone, and then he would go from room to room, looking behind doors and into closets, until he was satisfied in his own mind that there was no woman in the house. After that, he would feel better. He could then go back to his own house with a calm mind.

But Elam was away again for the week-end, and Max could not sit still. He could not eat his meals, and he could not sleep. He sat beside his window looking across to the western slope, his window raised several inches in case there should be the sound of an automobile in the intervale. He sat by the window all day Saturday, Saturday evening, and Sunday.

Late Sunday afternoon, when Max knew it was time for Elam to come back home, he heard Elam's automobile coming up the intervale. He knew it was Elam's car, and he knew he could not sit there another minute. He jumped up and found his hat and coat and started down the front doorstep.

The road was not within sight of Max's house, as there was a grove of birch trees down there, and he could not see the automobile. He heard Elam drive into his lane, however, and he waited and listened until the sound of the motor stopped abruptly in the barn.

There was something about the abruptness of the sound's stopping that caused him to pause on the doorstep. The motor was shut off the moment the car entered the barn, and then there was complete silence again in the intervale. Not even the rumbling sound of Elam closing the barn doors could be heard. Max wondered if Elam could be in such a hurry to get into his house that he had not waited to close the barn doors. He could not think of any reason to explain that. A man who was in such a great hurry to get into his house would certainly have something of importance coming up. Max thought about that, but he could think of no reason why a man would fail to close the barn doors.

He sat down on the doorstep and waited. He turned his head from side to side, allowing each ear to try to detect some sound in the intervale. Surely, he thought to himself, Elam had not gone and lost his mind. But he could think of no other reason for Elam's failure to close the barn doors. A man who drove his automobile into the barn and then left the doors open would certainly be foolish, and Elam had not been known theretofore as a foolish man. Elam knew better than to leave the barn doors open when evening was coming.

The sun in the intervale was dim and gray. A bank of gray clouds had risen in the northwest, and before long there would be no more sunshine. It was after three o'clock then, and the sun had already set on the western slope. Max had become accustomed to two o'clock sunsets on the eastern slope of the intervale, but when it set before three o'clock on the western slope, he was unprepared for it.

During all the time that he had been sitting on his doorstep, Max had hoped that Elam would come over to see him and tell him about the trip to Lewiston. Elam had always done that. Each time Elam had gone away for the week end in Lewiston, he had come home Sunday afternoon, had slammed shut the barn doors, and then had walked down the lane and up the slope and told Max what he had seen and what he had done in Lewiston. It was long past the time for him to come, and he had not even closed the barn doors. Max could not sit still and wait for Elam any longer. He got up and started down the slope towards the road.

When he reached the road, he stopped a moment and looked up towards Elam's farm and buildings. The barn door was wide open, and the automobile stood there exposed to the weather. There was no one to be seen about the house, but the shades had been opened, and the entrance door was ajar. Something was wrong, Max thought. Something had happened to Elam this time on his trip to Lewiston.

Standing beside Elam's mail box, Max looked up the slope towards the house. It was only a few hundred yards away, and he could see everything as plainly as if he had been standing on the doorstep. The white paint was whiter than ever in the gray twilight of the intervale, and the green trim was brighter than the grass in midsummer. Max stood looking at the place, waiting.

He had been staring at the house for ten minutes without seeing a single sign of Elam, when suddenly Elam appeared at one of the windows. He raised the window with a single thrust of his arm, and stuck out his head. Immediately another window was raised, on the opposite corner of the house, and a woman stuck out her head. They looked at each other for a moment, and then both withdrew their heads and the windows were lowered so quickly that Max was certain that the glass had been cracked. For a few seconds he did not believe what his eyes had seen. He would not believe that he had actually seen a woman in Elam's house. But slowly the realization came to him that he had seen a woman there, a young woman with a full body and yellow hair, and he stepped backward off Elam's land into the public road.

After what he had seen, Max did not know whether to stand there looking at the house, or whether to turn and go back up the slope to his own place. He knew he would never again set foot on Elam's land, however; he had already made up his mind never to have anything more to do with Elam Stairs. He did not even wish to speak to him again. He could never forgive Elam for having brought home a woman from Lewiston.

While he stood in the road trying to make up his mind about what he was going to do, the woman he had first seen in the window came running around the corner of the house. Max stared unbelievingly. Then a moment later came Elam, running faster than Max thought it possible for anyone to run. He was overtaking the yellow-haired young woman, two strides to her one, and if they had not turned the other corner of the house at that moment, he would have seen Elam grab her. Elam had his coat off, and the woman's dress was open down her back all the way to her waist. The woman was laughing, but Elam was not.

Max waited another five minutes, wishing to be there in case they again ran around the house. Then he turned and walked slowly up the eastern slope of the intervale. The sight of a woman at Elam's house made him wish to go over there and drive her out of the intervale, but he knew he could never do that. Elam would not allow him to run her away. Elam would protect her, and send him back across the road.

By the time that Max had reached his own house, he had definitely made up his mind about what he was going to do. He was going to take a trip himself the following week-end. He was going down to Lewiston Saturday morning and stay there until Sunday afternoon. And while he was there he would do the same things that Elam had done.

"Elam Stairs isn't the only man in the intervale who can bring home a woman," he said, taking his seat beside the window and looking over at the western slope where the sun had set. He raised the window several inches so that he might hear any sound that was audible in the intervale. "Will hire me a housekeeper in Lewiston and bring her back here, too. Elam Stairs has an hour's more sunshine because his farm and buildings are on the western slope, and he thinks he can have even more advantage with a housekeeper. But he shan't. I'll show him that I can go to Lewiston and maybe get a finer-looking housekeeper than he's got."

Max hitched his chair closer to the window.

"Guess I'll chase mine thrice around the house when I bring her here," he said. "And it might be a good plan to wait till she gets right in the middle of changing her clothes to start chasing her, instead of starting after her like Elam did when she only had her dress unfastened down her back. Guess Elam Stairs will see as how I made a pretty smart deal, when he looks out his window some fine day and sees me chasing a naked housekeeper, and gaining on her three strides to her one. He chased his woman once around the house, so I'll chase mine thrice around, with maybe an extra time to show him what I can do when I get good and started."

Max paused to look out across the intervale. While he watched Elam's house, he began going through the motions of washing his hands.

"Don't guess Elam's idea was so bad, after all. Can't think of much to quarrel about with a Lewiston young woman in the house, and not having to pay her five-ten dollars for her bed over the week end."

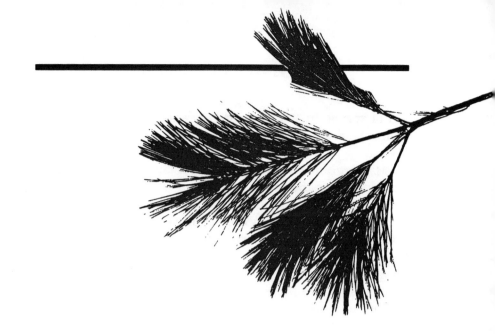

THE AUTOMOBILE
THAT WOULDN'T RUN

Mal Anderson made himself comfortable beside his dog on the back seat of the automobile and tuned up his banjo. Signe sat in a rocking chair on the front porch of the Penobscot Hotel listening to the music Mal made. It was midsummer and the weather was hot. It looked as if a thunderstorm might come from the west before the afternoon was over. Occasionally a gust of wind did come from that direction, blowing the dust down the street in balls like little yellow balloons.

Mal had a job in the spool mill in summer but he did not like to work the year 'round. He went into the woods in winter and did not come out until spring. In the summer he wanted to live in his shack with the dog and play his banjo when Signe sat on the hotel porch.

Mal strummed away on his banjo. Signe sat on the porch rocking faster and faster.

Plunkety plunk . . . plunkety plunk . . . plunkety plink!

Mal, who was called by everybody who did not like him "that damn Swede," was a fine woodsman. In the spool mill, though, he was not such a good workman. He did not like to work in the mill in summer. The mill made spools for electric wires, and Mal was supposed to be there now, checking the squares before they went through the turning-machines; but he did not like to work the year 'round.

Signe ran the Penobscot Hotel. It was a woodsman's hotel. The men used it when they came to town to spend the money they made up in the woods. Signe ran the hotel without help. She did not need any.

Plunkety plunk . . . plunkety plunk . . . plunkety plink!

Mal played his banjo for Signe. Neither of them ever spoke to the other. Mal might just as well have been born without the power of speech, for all the use he made of it. A man could talk to him an hour and he would not say a word.

Signe went to the kitchen and brought back a bone for Mal's dog. Mal opened the door and the dog jumped out after the bone and hopped in again. The dog curled up on the seat beside Mal and licked the bone. Mal played a tune on his banjo for Signe.

Plunkety plunk . . . plunkety plunk . . . plunkety plink!

At five o'clock Signe went into the hotel to start supper. Mal laid his banjo on the seat and he and the dog got out and pushed the automobile up the street to the shed beside his shack. The car would not run. One winter while Mal was up in the woods somebody broke into the shed and took the engine out. When Mal came back in the spring, he got into the habit of pushing his automobile to the hotel where he played his banjo for Signe.

Mal pushed his automobile up the street to the shed. His boss was there waiting to see him. Mal did not like him at all.

"Hello there, Mal," Scott, the boss, said. "I got some good news for you."

"I don't want to hear your news."

Mal knew that when Scott came to the shack he wanted to get some more work out of him. Nobody in the woods liked Scott.

"Get your stuff together, Mal. We're pushing up into the woods tomorrow morning at four o'clock."

"To hell with you and the woods and all your damn spools," Mal shouted, slamming shut the shed door. The only way to make Mal talk was to get him angry. But it was dangerous to make him mad. He had run half a dozen boss woodsmen out of the country. They went to Canada before he got a chance to hurt them.

Scott went down the road without looking back once. Scott was a brave boss woodsman.

Mal went into his shack and slammed shut the door behind him. The dog curled up under the table waiting for supper.

Everybody in the woods had heard about Mal Anderson. He was the best banjo player between Rangeley and Caribou, for one thing. And he was one of the best woodsmen ever to lay a tree down in the woods. He could stick a stake in the ground where he wanted the tree to fall and make the tree drive the stake into the earth. He took his two axes and went to work. When one ax became too hot he laid it aside and took up the other one. Give any two men the same start on a tree with a saw, axes, or anything they wanted, and Mal would have his tree on the ground before the other one was ready to fall. That was one reason why Mal was paid for eight days' work a week while the other men were getting paid for six.

It was summertime now and Mal did not want to go into the woods until winter. In summer he liked to stay in town and play his banjo in front of the Penobscot Hotel. The spool mill was running short of squares, however, and Mal had to help get the logs out of the woods. It was a hell of a time of year to make a man work.

Mal went up the river with the crew the next morning and went to work the following day felling trees for squares. He left his dog and banjo at home.

The crew worked in the woods three weeks and then the men began to grumble. When they left town, Scott had said they would be back by the end of two weeks. At the end of the third week Mal got mad. Scott was going to keep them there another month. And long before the end of the fourth week Scott had to watch himself pretty closely. He had to watch himself to keep from getting hurt. For instance, a tree might fall on him.

"Let's sink the son of a bitch in the river," one of the woodsmen suggested.

"Tie him to a stump and let the bobcats have him," another said. "You couldn't drown the yellow-backed bastard; he was born like a bullfrog."

"Mal'll catch him under a tree some of these days," Sanderson, who was the head teamster, said. "Let Mal have him."

Mal sat back on his haunches and said nothing.

Scott had enough sense to go into his shack every night after supper and not show himself until daylight. He could have been finished in five minutes in the dark, and he knew it.

But at the end of six weeks Scott was in as good condition as he had ever been. He watched himself pretty closely in the woods and he did not show himself after dark.

In the meantime two of the men got it into their heads that they were going out of the woods, Scott or no Scott. They said nothing about it and got ready to slip out alone. Scott was in his shack washing up for dinner when they ran down to the river and pushed off in a canoe.

Scott missed them a few minutes later when everybody sat down at the table to eat. Calling Mal and another man, they ran down to the river. The two men who had set their heads on going out of the woods were half a mile downstream paddling like mad. They were standing up in the canoe on the lookout for submerged logs and rocks. Their arms and paddles waved like a windmill in a cyclone.

"Get a canoe, Mal, and pick out a good man to help you and bring those God-damn Canucks back to me," Scott ordered, swearing and stamping around on the riverbank.

Mal motioned to one of the men nearest him and they shoved off without a word. Mal was the biggest and strongest man in camp. The other man was to help with the canoe.

The river lay in a straight course downstream for two miles or more. It was used for running logs to the spool mill in the spring and summer. In winter it was frozen over to a depth of three or four feet and the logging teams drove over it going and coming to the woods.

Scott sent a man to camp for his field glasses.

Mal and the other woodsman struck out down the river after the two runaway men. In both canoes the men worked frantically with their oars. Mal's canoe shot through the water at a terrific rate of speed. There was no doubt that he would overtake the other canoe within the next mile. He and the man in the stern squatted on their knees so they would be nearer the water. Their canoe shot down the river, leaving a foaming white wake spreading out to the shores behind.

The man came running back from camp with the field glasses for Scott.

"I'll break those God-damn Canucks of wanting to run away from the job," Scott shouted, snatching the glasses from the man's hand.

The two canoes looked only a dozen lengths apart now. The leading canoe was about a mile and a quarter downstream. Mal's canoe closed up on it with every powerful stroke of his blade. Scott thrust the glasses to his eyes and held them there. The woodsmen crowded down to the edge of the water straining their eyes to see Mal overtake the men. It would be a sight worth seeing. What he would probably do would be to hold their heads under the water until they were nearly drowned before hauling them into his canoe and bringing them back to Scott. Scott had already planned enough work to take all the fight out of them.

Mal's canoe closed up on the one that had had the first start. The men in the canoe were still paddling with all their might, but Mal was stroking faster and faster.

The next instant the two canoes were prow-and-prow, only an oar's length apart. And then, before anybody could see what had happened, Mal had passed them and the first canoe was a whole length behind.

"The God-damn son of a bloody—" Scott swore, smashing the field glasses against the rocks. He was so mad he was almost speechless. Mal had double-crossed him. He shouted at the men and kicked savagely at the broken field glasses on the shore. "The God-damn son of a bloody—" he shouted from the depths of his powerful lungs.

Both canoes were completely out of sight now. One canoe was actually half a mile ahead of the other.

Scott ordered the men back to the woods. After they had gone he walked slowly up the hillside to the camp. Mal Anderson had put one over on him.

Mal got home early the next afternoon and opened the door of his shack. His dog was sleeping under the shack and woke up when he sniffed Mal's scent inside. Mal made a fire and cooked something for the dog and himself to eat.

After they had finished eating Mal got his banjo and pushed his automobile out of the shed and down the street as far as the Penobscot Hotel. Signe was sitting on the front porch rocking in her chair. When she saw Mal coming down the street with his automobile, she leaned back in her chair and rocked faster and faster.

Mal pushed the car down the street and stopped it in front of Signe's hotel. He opened the door and he and the dog got into the back seat and sat down. Mal slammed shut the door and picked up his banjo. Then he began playing a tune for Signe.

The dog curled up and went to sleep. Mal strummed away on the banjo.

Plunkety plunk . . . plunkety plunk . . . plunkety plink!

Signe rocked back and forth, smiling out into the street at Mal sitting in his car and glad he was back in town again.

Mal settled down and propped his feet on the back of the driver's seat. Signe brought a bone for the dog and Mal opened the door. The dog jumped out after the bone and hopped in again and began licking it. Mal slammed shut the automobile door and took up his banjo again.

Plunkety plunk . . . plunkety plunk . . . plunkety plink!

The tune floated to the porch of the Penobscot Hotel and up the street and down it.

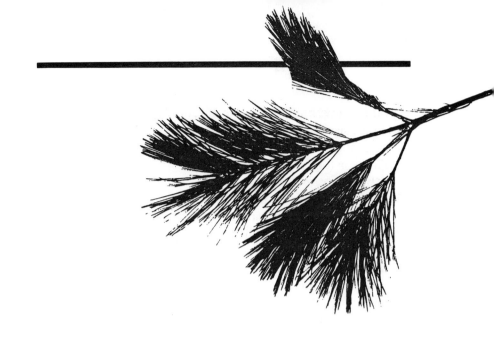

BALM OF GILEAD

Back in January, about the middle of the first week, Ned Jones received a letter from the fire insurance agent's office in Bangor. The letter said that the company, effective January 1st, last, had discontinued allowing a discount on premiums covering farmhouses and barns which were equipped with lightning rods. Therefore, the letter said, the cost for protection on his buildings would be raised to twenty-two-fifty from twenty-fifty.

However, the letter went on, if the rods were already installed on the building, a lightning-rod expert would call and inspect the terminals, ground wires, brads, and so forth, and if the expert found them in first-class condition, the discount would be reinstated. The charge for all of this, the letter concluded, would be three dollars for the inspector's time.

"Thunderation," Ned said when he had finished reading the letter the third time. "Hell and thunderation!"

It did not take him long to figure out that he would save a dollar by not having the lightning rods inspected, but even so he could see that it was going to cost him two dollars a year more to keep his buildings covered by insurance.

"That's thunderation," he said.

His wife, Betty, was silent about the whole matter. She always froze up inside whenever something came up like that and threatened to cost an extra penny.

The insurance premium was not due and payable until February 1st, but a week before that time Ned got ready to make a trip to Bangor and pay a call at the insurance agent's office.

He and his wife started out to Bangor after breakfast, driving the old car slowly along the black-top road, taking care to stay as far on the right-hand side of the road as possible. The law was that a car owner would not have to carry liability and property-damage insurance as long as he did not have a mishap. Ned was set on not having that first accident on the highways that would force him to pay insurance premiums for the right to drive his car. It was an old car anyway, about twelve years old, and he did not intend buying another one when it was worn out.

They got to Bangor just before ten o'clock in the forenoon, and, after finding a safe place to park and leave the automobile, Ned and his wife went straight to the agent's office.

They sat down on a bench in the hall and waited for several minutes, and then a girl took them to see Mr. Harmsworth.

"Now, about that insurance on my stand of buildings out at Gaylord," Ned said, shaking his head and his finger at the agent.

"I take it you're upset about the new lightning-rod clause, effective January 1st, last," Mr. Harmsworth said, smiling at Ned and his wife. "You see, Mr. Jones, and Mrs. Jones, the company at the home office in New Hampshire rewrites the contracts, and we agents have nothing whatever to do with the terms the company dictates."

"What do people in New Hampshire know about lightning rods anyway?" Ned said. "Now let me tell you. I once knew a man in New Hampshire who—"

"Let's not get off the subject, Mr. Jones, and Mrs. Jones," Mr. Harmsworth said. "After all, both my parents were born and raised in New Hampshire, and I'm sure there is a New Hampshire connection somewhere in your family, too."

He smiled at Mrs. Jones, beaming upon her all the force of what he knew was a sunny smile. Betty refused to be disarmed. She was frozen up inside, and she intended to remain unthawed as long as the insurance company refused to make an adjustment that would not cost them an extra penny.

"Now, I've lived down here in the State of Maine for all my life," Ned said, "and I'm sixty and more right now, and lightning rods are the only things in the world that'll keep lightning from striking and setting fire to the house or barn. All my life I've seen lightning strike a spire and run down the cable into the ground without even so much as smoking up the roof and clapboards. If it wasn't for lightning rods—"

"Are you sure lightning runs down lightning rods, Mr. Jones, and Mrs. Jones?" Mr. Harmsworth said. "I was under the impression it ran up the rods, or rather made contact on the point of the spire. However—"

"Lightning is lightning, whether it runs up or down, or slantwise, if it has a mind to," Ned said, rising up.

"I see you know a lot more about such things than I do," Mr. Harmsworth laughed, beaming upon Mrs. Jones. "I was raised here in the city, and I never had a chance to observe how lightning behaves when it comes in contact with a rod-equipped building. But, just the same, there's nothing either you or I can do about this here clause, because the home office rewrote the contract and sent us the printed forms, and I'm merely their representative. I carry out their orders, but I have no authority to alter a clause in a contract."

Ned looked at his wife, and she shook her head. That was all he wanted to know. No insurance company, with a home office in New Hampshire, run by New Hampshire people, was going to tell him whether they thought lightning rods were protection or not. He looked at his wife again, and shook his head. Betty tightened her mouth, freezing tighter inside, and nodded at Ned.

Mr. Harmsworth shuffled some papers on his desk, and, bringing one out with much crinkling and creasing, laid it before Ned.

"This is your bill for fire-protection coverage, due February 1st," he said, glancing quickly at Ned, but not looking at Mrs. Jones.

Ned pushed it back at him.

"Now, about this Balm of Gilead," Ned said, edging forward in his chair.

"What Balm of Gilead?" Mr. Harmsworth asked, startled. "What's that?"

Ned looked at his wife, and Betty nodded. That was what he wanted to know from her. He pulled his chair closer to the desk.

"My Balm of Gilead," he said. "I've got one in my dooryard, fourteen feet from the west wall of my dwelling house, and twenty-two feet from the east wall of my barn."

"What's a Balm of Gilead?" Mr. Harmsworth asked, still startled. "Wasn't that something in the Bible? How'd you get something that was in the Bible?"

Ned and Betty looked at each other, but neither of them made any motion of the head.

"Balm of Gilead is a tree," Ned said. "My Balm of Gilead was set out by my father, seventy-seven years ago, and it stands in my dooryard."

"What about it?" Mr. Harmsworth asked, wild-eyed.

"It's a lightning rod," Ned said. "It's the finest lightning rod on earth. After a Balm of Gilead—"

"You want us to give you a discount because you have a tree—" Mr. Harmsworth began, sitting forward in his chair.

"—passes its fiftieth year, it turns into a lightning rod," Ned continued doggedly. "Lightning won't strike any other thing within fifty yards of it. Lightning strikes the Balm of Gilead every time."

"I don't know what you're driving at exactly," Mr. Harmsworth said, "but I wouldn't suppose you expect to get any discount on your fire insurance for having a tree like that."

Betty stiffened her backbone.

"I don't know why not," Ned said. "Why shouldn't I get a discount when I've got a Balm of Gilead located almost halfway between my two buildings, and the farthest is twenty-two feet from it. A tree like that is two or three times more protection than rods on the buildings. Why, it even makes the buildings proof against lightning! I figure I'm due five or six dollars discount for having that tree where it is."

Mr. Harmsworth scratched his head and took a swift look at Mrs. Jones. He had time to see that her mouth was drawn in a tight line across her face. He did not look at her again.

"If you insist upon it," he said, "I'll take it up with the home office in New Hampshire. I won't be able to do a thing until I hear from them. But I shouldn't think they would allow anybody a discount on fire insurance for having a Balm of Gilead tree."

"If they wasn't those New Hampshire people," Ned said, "they'd know how much protection a tree like that is."

"I'll write you a letter and let you know what the home office has to say just as soon as I get their answer," he said, standing up.

Ned and Betty got up and went out into the hall. Mr. Harmsworth followed them trying to shake hands with at least one of them. Betty kept her hands clasped tightly across her waist. Ned outwalked the agent to the street.

"Ignorant young cuss," Ned said. "Associates with New Hampshire people."

Betty nodded her head.

They bought a few things in a store, and then got into their car and drove home. Neither of them mentioned the insurance during the rest of the day.

During the remainder of the week, and through the first three days of the following one, both Ned and his wife watched the mail for the letter from the agent in Bangor. On the third day the letter came.

They went into the kitchen and sat down in the chairs by the window before opening it. Ned first took out his glasses and carefully polished the lenses. Betty put her handkerchief to her nose, and then put it away. Ned read the letter aloud.

> DEAR MR. JONES:
> I have taken up the matter of the Balm of Gilead tree in your dooryard with the home office in New Hampshire, and I am herewith advising you of their decision. It seems that the company thought it was all a joke or something because, in their own words, they wished to know if your Balm of Gilead tree would "catch mice, scare crows away, and cure painter's colic." Further along in their letter they state most emphatically that under no circumstances would a discount on fire-insurance premiums be allowed for possession of a Balm of Gilead tree. . . .

The letter did not end there, but Ned read no farther. He handed the letter to his wife, and she laid it aside on the table, drawing her mouth into a thin straight line across her face.

"I never did waste any feelings for the people of New Hampshire," Ned said, putting away his glasses, getting his hat, and standing up.

His wife did not say a word when he left the kitchen and went out into the dooryard.

Balm of Gilead

When she saw him come out of the woodshed with the ax and the crosscut saw, she put on her jacket and went out to help him.

First he cut a notch in the Balm of Gilead on the side in order to fell it in the direction where he wanted it to fall. When that was done, he picked up one end of the crosscut, and Betty picked up the other end. They began sawing silently, their faces bright but drawn in tight lines, and both hoping that an electrical storm would come early in the spring, and each of them praying silently that lightning would strike the house and burn it to a heap of ashes on the ground.

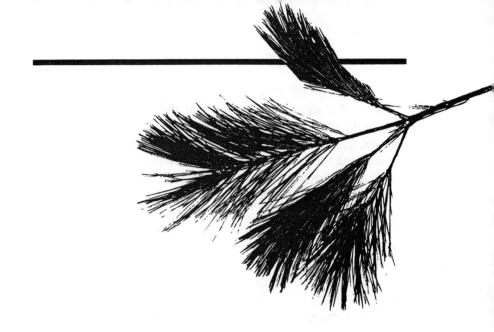

AN AUTUMN
COURTSHIP

Amos Williams had been carrying a jug of his last
year's cider over to Esther Tibbetts' every Sunday
night for two months or more and he thought it
was about time for something to happen. Amos
had been trying all summer to marry Esther, but
Esther owned a good farm and a fine set of buildings and she thought she was very well off just as
she was. Every Sunday night Esther seemed to be
ready to say she would marry Amos, but by that
time the cider was all gone and he had to go
away and wait for another week to pass before he
could try again.

When he went back to work at the skewer-mill Monday morning the other men wanted to know if anything had happened the night before. Everybody in the mill knew that Amos was trying his hardest to marry Esther before winter and cold weather came. Amos had begun taking Esther a jug of cider because one of the men there had said that if a woman drank enough cider she would marry anybody.

"What did Esther say last night, Amos?" one of the men asked him, winking at the others. "Did she say she would get married to you?"

Amos said nothing for a few minutes. The mill was turning out candy-sticks for all-day suckers this week because there was a big stock of meat-skewers on hand and a large order for candy-sticks had been received over the week-end. Amos picked up a wrench and adjusted the turning-machine on his bench while everybody stood around waiting to hear about Esther.

"The cider gave out too quick, I guess," he said. "I thought for a while she was going to say she would get married, but I guess there wasn't enough cider."

"What you should do, Amos," another of the men said seriously, "is to take two jugs of cider with you next Sunday night. When I was courting my wife I couldn't do a thing with her until I began taking two jugs with me when I went to see her. You should take two jugs of cider, Amos. That will make things happen, all right."

"I'll have to do something about it," Amos said. "My cider-barrel is getting low. I've only got five or six gallons left in it now. And winter is coming on, too. If Esther don't marry me pretty soon, I'll have to buy some new blankets."

"You take Esther two jugs next Sunday night, Amos, and if all that cider won't make something happen for you I'll give you five gallons out of my own barrel."

Amos pulled the belt on his machine and went to work turning candy-sticks. He was getting uneasy now that winter was coming. He had planned to marry Esther before it began to be cold at night so he would not have to buy any new blankets. His sister had taken all his quilts when she was married that past spring and now he could not get them away from her. Esther had a lot of quilts and if he could marry her they would use hers that winter. Everything would work out just fine if Esther would only say she would marry him. He would live in Esther's house because it was a mile closer to the skewer-mill than his own, and he would not have to walk so far when he went to work.

By the end of the week Amos was desperate. Since Tuesday there had been a heavy frost every night and the only bed-covering he had was the old yellow quilt his sister said she would not have. It would have been a foolish waste of money to go to the store and buy two or three sets of blankets, considering the fact that Esther had dozens and dozens of quilts which they would use if she would only marry him before winter and cold weather came.

Early Sunday evening Amos filled two jugs with his last-year's cider and took them with him to see Esther. When he got there he wanted Esther to begin drinking with him right away. Esther liked cider, especially when it was a year old, and they drank one jug empty before nine o'clock. Amos had not said a word the whole evening about marrying. He figured that it would be better to wait and talk about that when they started on the second jug.

Esther took a good drink from the new jug and danced a few steps before she sat down again.

"This is good cider, Esther," he said preliminarily.

Esther put her hand over her mouth and swallowed two or three times in quick succession.

"You always have good apple-juice, Amos," she smiled at him.

Amos rubbed the palms of his hands nervously over his knees, trying to erase the indigo stain of white birch from the skin. He liked to hear Esther praise his cider.

"The boys at the skewer-mill promised to give me a whole barrel of cider when I get married," he lied shamelessly.

He glanced at Esther, hoping to find on her face some sign of the effect the carefully planned story should have had on her. Esther looked blankly at the ceiling, as though she did not know why Amos came to see her every Sunday night with his last-year's cider. Amos poured her another glass from the jug.

While she drank the cider, Amos studied the pile of thick quilts and comforters on the foot of her bed in the next room. Seeing Esther's quilts made him more than ever determined to marry her right away. He could see no sense in his coming to her house every week and bringing her his good cider when, if she would marry him, he could be there every night and have all his cider for himself.

And this time, when he brought two jugs, he knew he had the best opportunity of his life. If Esther drank both jugs of cider and still continued to say that she would not marry him, then there would be no use in wasting any more of his cider on her.

Esther finished the glass and gave it to Amos. He put it on the table and turned around just in time to see Esther lifting her skirt near the hem with a thumb and forefinger and carelessly throwing one leg across the other. He knew at once that the second jug was doing all it should do, because Esther had never crossed her legs so gayly during all the other times he had been bringing one jug. He poured her another glass, and rubbed his birch-stained hands together enthusiastically while she was placing the glass to her lips.

"Esther, I've got more than seven thousand dollars in the savings-bank," he began. That was the first thing he said each time he asked her to marry him. "My farm and buildings are worth three thousand dollars, and I haven't any debts."

Esther lifted her eyelids and looked at Amos. Her eyes were sleepy-looking but she was wide awake.

"I don't want to be married," she said, beginning to giggle a little for the first time. "I want to stay like I am, Amos."

This was the only time he had ever been with Esther when she had a cider-giggle. He watched her anxiously, startled by her prompt refusal.

"But blankets—" he cried out nervously.

"What blankets?" she asked, raising herself on her elbow and guiding herself across the room. The cider-giggle was getting beyond her control.

"Winter is coming—cold weather!" he shouted desperately.

"What about cold weather, Amos?" she giggled again.

"I was just thinking about blankets," he said hopelessly.

Esther went to the door and looked into her bedroom. Amos came and stood behind her.

"I haven't any blankets, Amos," she giggled, "but I've got a lot of quilts and comforters."

Amos looked hopefully over her shoulder at the pile of quilts and comforters on her bed.

"I want us to get married, Esther," he said thickly. "How would you like to marry me?"

Esther pushed Amos roughly aside and went back into the room. She was giggling so foolishly she could not speak.

Amos went to the table and poured her another glass of cider. While she drank it he glanced at the almost empty jug, realizing that he would have to hurry Esther if he was to get her consent before all the cider was gone.

When she handed him the empty glass, Amos put it on the table and caught her hands before she could jerk away from him. Then, holding her arms so she could not push him away, he kissed her. Knowing that she would try to push him away when he did that, he put his arms around her and held her while he talked to her about marrying him.

"I want that you should marry me, Esther," he struggled with her strength, "because if you don't I'll have to buy some blankets for the winter."

Esther pushed and scratched but Amos held her all the tighter. He could see that she was mad, but at the same time she could not keep from giggling just as sillily as ever. Amos poured out the last glass of cider for her while he held her with one hand.

Still holding her with one hand he tried to force the cider into her mouth. Suddenly she shoved Amos with all her might, and both of them fell on the floor. Amos was not hurt, but Esther struck her knee on a chair and cut a deep gash in her leg. The blood ran through her stocking and dripped on the floor beside them.

"Esther, I want that you should marry me right away before—" he began a second time.

Before he could say another word Esther had grabbed the nearest cider-jug and hit him over the head with it. The blow was glancing, and the jug only stunned him for a moment. She had swung the jug so hard, though, that it was jerked from her fingers and crashed against the cast-iron stove. She immediately reached for the second jug, but Amos was too quick for her. He ran to the door and out into the yard before she could throw it at him. When he got to the road, she had reached the door, and with all her strength she hurled the stone jug at Amos. Amos dodged out of the way and ran down the road toward his house.

When he got home there was nothing to do but drink some cider and go to bed. He was so mad about the way things turned out that he drank almost three times as much cider as he usually did when he went down into his cellar.

By the time Amos started to the skewer-mill the next morning he was resigned to his inability to marry Esther. His only regrets now were that he had wasted all his last-year's cider on her and would have to buy two or three sets of blankets, after all.

When he got to the mill a stranger was standing in the doorway. The man made no effort to move when Amos tried to enter.

"Your name is Amos Williams, isn't it?" he asked.

"Amos Williams it's been ever since I can remember," Amos said sourly, trying to get into the mill.

"Well, you will have to come along with me to the county jail," he said, holding out a folded paper.

"What for?" Amos demanded.

"The paper says 'Assault on the Person of Esther Tibbetts.' "

The man who had promised Amos five gallons of cider the week before, when he suggested that Amos take Esther two jugs, came up the road to the mill door. He asked Amos what the trouble was and Amos told him.

"You got me into all this trouble," Amos swore at him. "You said two jugs would make her marry me, and now she's had me arrested for assault."

"Well, it's too bad you've got to go to jail and lose all that time here at the mill, Amos, but it was all your own fault."

"How was it my fault?"

"It's like this, Amos. There are three kinds of women. There are one-jug, two-jug, and three-jug women. You should have told me at the start that Esther was a three-jug woman. If you had done that, I could have told you to take her three jugs of cider instead of only two."

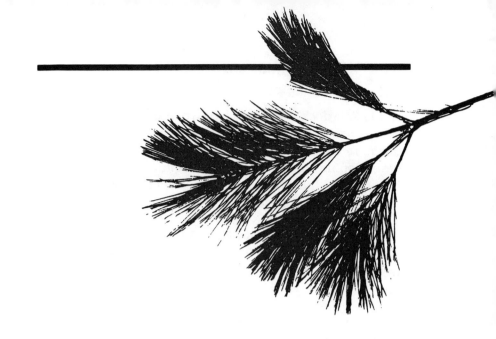

THE WINDFALL

When Waldo Murdock, whose trade, when he felt like working at it, was rendering creatures, came into the unexpected inheritance, there had been no commotion in Brighton to equal it since the time when, eleven years before, one of the Perkins brothers, with no more forewarning than a stroke of summer lightning, ran away in broad daylight with the resident minister's wife.

As for the townspeople, none of them, not even Aunt Susie Shook, who told fortunes by reading tea leaves, or coffee grounds if necessary, had ever had the remotest idea that anything in the nature of sudden wealth would fall into

Waldo Murdock's scrawny lap, while at the same time, of course, people were quick to say that if he had not been sitting down, as usual, instead of being up and doing, there would have been no lap of his for it to fall into; and certainly Waldo himself, even though he daydreamed about almost everything else under the sun, had never entertained such a far-fetched thought in his mind.

Waldo did not even know he had a brother in Australia and, even if he had known it, he would never have imagined that he would be remembered in a will. From Bangor to Burlington, all the Murdocks, especially the home-owning branch of the family, were known throughout the entire region north of Boston for their trait, which relatives by marriage and other outsiders called cussedness, of not acknowledging kinship with one another. And as it was, it was all Waldo could do to force himself, after having cast aside pride of long standing, publicly to admit blood relationship with another Murdock, even if he had lived in Australia, long enough to go to the bank in Waterville and cash the check the lawyer from Portland had handed him.

"Pay no mind to what the people say," he told the clerk in the bank. "There may be others in the State of Maine bearing the name of Murdock, but there's not a single drop of mingling blood that I would own to. I'd sooner claim kinship with my old black cow than I would with a so-called Murdock."

Dessie, Waldo's wife, was, at the beginning, the most level-headed of all. She maintained her mental balance, if only at the start, much better than Waldo and some of the townspeople. Dessie, although afterward she regretted not having gone along, even remained at home and tended the house chores while Waldo was away in Waterville cashing the check. There was only one thing she did out of the ordinary that forenoon, and that was to make Justine, the hired girl, air the parlor and shake out the scatter rugs, even if it was not Saturday.

During all that time the neighbors were ringing her up on the phone and asking what she was going to do with all that money, but that, too, in the beginning, failed to veer the even measure of her thoughts.

"When the check is cashed, if it's not worthless, and it'll be a wonder if it's not, there'll be ample time at hand for me to go out of my way to think about it," she told them. "Right now, and likely forever after, it's nothing but a scrawl and a promise on a slip of paper."

Dessie went back to work with her lips a little tighter each time she finished talking to one of the neighbors on the phone. She was not exactly worried, she told Justine, but she was feeling impatient. Waldo failed to come home at the noon hour for dinner, and it was not long after that before she, like everybody else in Brighton who was working himself into a frenzy over Waldo's sudden windfall, began thinking of the things that could be done with the money.

Late that afternoon Waldo drove up to the dooryard and left the automobile standing there instead of putting it away in the shed where it belonged.

Justine came running to tell her.

Dessie was so on edge by that time that she jumped several inches off the chair seat when Justine, who was as excited as she by then, ran into the room where she was.

"Mr. Murdock's back!" Justine cried, twisting her fingers.

"He'd better be!" Dessie said. "If he hadn't got home when he did, he could have just kept on traveling, for all the concern I'd ever have."

"I guess Mr. Murdock has the real money," Justine said, looking over her shoulder. "He looked like he was feeling good about it when he got out of the auto."

Dessie leaped to her feet.

"Go on about your tasks, whatever they be, Justine," she said crossly. "It's none of your money, if there is any, anyway."

Justine went to the kitchen and watched Waldo come along the path to the side door.

Waldo came in, throwing his hat on the table. He looked at Dessie for a moment, cocking his head a little to one side. His coat pocket sagged heavily.

Neither Dessie nor Waldo spoke for a while.

Presently Dessie walked up to him and held out her hand.

"Guess I'll take charge for the time being," she said stiffly. "Hand it over."

Waldo reached into his coat pocket, drawing out a mostly empty bottle and handing it to her. She stepped back, looking at it severely. Then, without a word, she grabbed the bottle by the neck and slung it with all her might across the room. It struck the wall, shattering into dozens of pieces.

"I might have known it, and I would have, if I had only had the sense God has given most people!" she said, raising her voice. "I've got only myself to blame!"

Waldo reached for a chair.

"Now there's no cause for a human to take on so, Dessie," he said. "Everything turned out, from here to there and back again, like it was made to order."

He reached into his pants pocket and drew out a bulging roll of greenbacks. The bills were tied tightly around the center with a piece of heavy twine. Dessie forgot her anger the instant she saw the money. The scowling lines on her face disappeared completely while she watched Waldo bounce the roll up and down in his hand.

"All I've got to say," she began, "is that I never thought I'd live to breathe the air of the day when a deceasing Murdock would have the decency to do the honorable thing with his money, even if he couldn't find means of taking it along with him when he went, which would be a wonder if he didn't try to do, and he probably did, anyway."

Waldo leaned back and let her talk to her heart's content. He felt so good himself that he wanted her to have a good time, too. He let her speak what came to mind, without uttering a single grumble.

— 44 —

"Have you any more blood relations that we've neglected to remind ourselves of, Waldo?" she asked, leaning toward him. "It seems to me that I recall your second cousin in Skowhegan saying once some years ago that a Murdock went to California at the end of the Spanish-American War and prospected for gold. It might be that he struck it rich out there, which a lot of people did, so I've read, if reading can be believed. If we'd been more particular about your blood relations in the past, we wouldn't have to sit here now and wrack our brains trying to call them to mind at a time like this."

"Guess I have no blood relations of the name of Murdock," Waldo said firmly.

Dessie drew a deep breath and looked longingly at the large roll of greenbacks bouncing up and down in her husband's hand.

Suddenly she leaned forward and grasped the roll desperately.

Waldo snatched it from her.

"I think we ought to start making plans," she said.

"This is Murdock money, woman," he said quickly. "A Murdock made it, and a Murdock shall spend it."

Dessie sat up decisively.

"Well, anyway, we'll be sensible," she said calmly. "We won't throw it away on trifles like a lot of people would who I could mention, if I had a mind to."

"I've got it all settled, Dessie," Waldo told her, smiling as a kindly feeling came over him. "Guess we can afford to have a good time now at our age. Maybe we won't be lingering here much longer, which would be a shame if we hadn't taken full advantage of it by the time we went. Wouldn't be no sense in hoarding it only to have to pass it along to somebody else after we are gone."

Dessie nodded approvingly, her spirits rising again.

"I've always wanted a fur neckpiece, Waldo," she said, her face bright with hope.

Dessie did not sleep a single wink that night. For an hour after they had gone to bed, she lay silently tense, listening. Waldo did not stir. He lay on his back listening to Dessie's labored breathing.

Just before midnight Dessie got up as quietly as she possibly could and tiptoed to the foot of the bed where Waldo had laid his pants over the back of a chair. It was dark in the room with the shades drawn, and she took care in feeling her way to the chair. She was trembling nervously when she touched it, and the jerking of her breath had started a pain in her chest. Without losing any more time she slid her hand into the pants pocket.

"Get your hand out of my pants, Dessie," Waldo said, rising up in bed. "Leave that money be."

Dessie dropped the pants without having touched the money, and went back to bed without a word. Neither of them spoke as she lay down again and tried to make herself as comfortable as possible for the remainder of the night. After that both of them lay staring into the blackness of the room.

Just as dawn was beginning to show the first signs of breaking, Dessie slid carefully from the bed and crawled on her hands and knees toward the chair. As she was rising up to reach the pants, Waldo sat up erectly.

"Don't want to have to mention it again about you putting your hand in my pants pocket," he said. "Leave that money be, Dessie."

Dessie dropped the pants and went to the window. She stood there watching a red dawn break in the east. After a while she began dressing, and as she was leaving the chamber she heard Justine starting a fire in the kitchen stove.

While she and Justine were preparing breakfast, she began to realize how uneasy she really was about the money. She had spent a sleepless night worrying over the wealth, and she was afraid she would not get a chance to spend a single penny of it herself.

"Mrs. Murdock," Justine said, coming and standing beside her, "Carl and I could get mated right away if we had the money for a chamber suite."

"Let Carl Friend make his own money," Dessie said sharply, turning on the girl. "Me and my husband have worked hard all our lives for what we possess. It won't hurt Carl Friend to do the same for you, if he wants a family."

"I couldn't sleep much last night for staying awake wondering if you and Mr. Murdock wouldn't want to help me out," Justine said persistently. "Especially because I've worked here for you six years without asking favors, and I didn't think you'd miss a little of all that big inheritance from Australia."

"Mind your own affairs, Justine!" she said sharply. "Besides, Carl Friend can get the money from his own family if he wants to furnish a house for you. Those Friends have made plenty of profit in roof tinning in the past."

"They won't help any, Mrs. Murdock," Justine said sadly. "And Carl and I don't want to have to wait and wait and wait."

"You don't have to hurry the marriage for any reason, do you?" Dessie asked suspiciously.

Justine looked at her for several moments, her thoughts racing through her mind.

"Not exactly," she admitted at last.

"Well, then," Dessie said, turning away, "in that case, you can afford to wait."

In turning abruptly she almost walked headlong into Waldo. He had come into the kitchen and was going toward the pantry. After Dessie had stepped out of the way, she watched him go into the pantry and pick up several cans off the shelf. He found an empty coffee can and left, going through the kitchen and out the door without a word being spoken. Dessie watched him leave, wondering what he was about to do. She went to the window and watched as he walked to the toolshed and came out a moment later carrying a spade. With the coffee can in one hand and the spade over his shoulder, he disappeared out of sight behind the barn.

It was not until almost ten minutes had passed that Dessie realized what Waldo was doing behind the barn.

Just as she was opening the door to run out there and observe him from the corner of the barn, Waldo walked into view. He came toward the house, carrying the spade but not the coffee can. Dessie's heart sank. He had buried the can, and the money with it, and she had failed to get out there in time to see where the wealth had been hidden. She walked back into the kitchen and placed breakfast on the table.

Waldo came in a few minutes later, washed his hands at the pump, and sat down at his place. He began eating as though nothing out of the ordinary had taken place out behind the barn. Neither she nor Waldo had anything to say to each other during the whole twenty minutes they were at the table. When he finished eating, he got up and put on his hat.

"Have some affairs to attend to in the village," he said shortly. "Will be away for the forenoon, the whole of it."

Dessie nodded. She had to grip her hands tightly in order to hide her impatience. She waited until Waldo had got out of sight, and then she grabbed Justine by the arm and pulled her through the door. Pushing Justine ahead, Dessie ran as fast as she could to the toolshed, where she quickly snatched up two spades, and then hurried toward the back of the barn.

She set Justine to digging right away, while she looked the ground over carefully, hoping to find evidence of a freshly covered hole. She searched for nearly half an hour without finding a single trace of the hole she was positive Waldo had dug, and after that she went to work, digging methodically.

After several hours, Justine slumped to the ground, completely exhausted. Dessie was tired, too, and the blisters on her hands made digging so painful that she could hardly bear to hold the spade. But she forced herself to keep on, allowing Justine to rest a few minutes.

"Get up and dig, Justine," she called breathlessly, not being able to bear seeing her idle any longer.

Justine crawled to her feet and tried to push the blade of her spade into the stony earth. She wanted to beg Dessie to let her rest some more, but when she glanced up and saw Dessie's closely clamped lips, she knew it would be useless to ask.

Dessie stopped for a moment to ease her back. When her eyes were raised from the ground, she saw Fred Paxton leaning over the stone wall beside the road a hundred feet away.

"Going fishing, Dessie?" he called. "See you're digging fishing worms."

Dessie thrust her hand against the small of her aching back and straightened up a little more.

"Thought I might," she said slowly. "It's been a long time since I went."

"Now that you and Waldo have all that money to falute on," Fred said, "I guess you and him can afford to spend all your time doing nothing but fish, if you have a mind to."

"Maybe," she said, tightening her lips.

The mere mention of the money inflamed her thoughts until she could not see clearly. She bent over the spade, thrusting the blade into the rough, stony ground with all her might. She kept doggedly at it until she was certain Fred had walked out of sight over the hill.

Later she sent Justine to the kitchen for some bread and potatoes left over from breakfast, and when Justine returned, Dessie sat down in the shade of the barn and ate hurriedly.

"While I was in the house, Mr. Murdock phoned and said he wouldn't be back in the forenoon," Justine said. "He told me to tell you he would be away in the afternoon, too, the whole of it."

Dessie leaped to her feet.

"Why didn't you tell me right away when you came back a minute ago?" she said angrily.

Justine glanced at the stony ground.

"We're not going to dig out here the whole afternoon, too, are we, Mrs. Murdock?" she inquired pleadingly. "My hands are raw with blisters, and—"

"Never mind that," Dessie said firmly. "We are going to dig this afternoon, the whole of it."

"But Mrs. Murdock—"

"Shut up, Justine, and do as you are told!"

When Dessie fell on the bed at dusk that evening, she had never before in all her life felt so thoroughly miserable. Not only had she spent the entire day digging in the stony ground behind the barn, but, moreover, she had not been able to find the coffee can. Her back felt as if she would never be able to use it again.

Once upon the bed, she moved her body carefully, easing herself into a prone position. Justine had gone out earlier in the evening with Carl Friend, and Waldo still had not returned. Dessie felt so tired and lonely that she wanted to cry. Just as she felt tears coming into her eyes, the phone began to ring. She lay motionless, listening to it ring for several minutes, hoping all the while that it would stop so she could begin crying.

The phone did not stop, and it sounded as if it never would as long as she lived. She got to her feet, pressing her hands over her ears in order to keep out the sound, and stumbled painfully to the hall. There she sat down in the chair beside the stand and lifted the receiver.

"Hello," she said unsteadily.

"Is this Waldo Murdock's wife?" a voice boomed.

"Yes," she answered, wondering who it could be.

"Then you'd better bestir yourself and fetch Waldo home where he belongs before it's too late. This is Charles Mason. Waldo is over here at my place, in the east part of town, annoying my household, and if he was a Democrat, I'd shoot him myself, instead of turning the job over to his wife. I've never in my life seen a man behave like he's doing. I guess it's public knowledge by now, otherwise I wouldn't be repeating it that sudden wealth has gone to his head, but that's still no excuse for the way he's doing."

"What's Waldo doing?" Dessie asked, shouting impulsively into the phone.

"He's befuddling Miss Wilson, the schoolteacher who boards at my house, into going away with him. He says he's going to set sail for Australia or somewhere."

"But he can't do that!" Dessie protested.

"That's what any average, normal, level-minded human being would think, too, but I don't know what's going to stop Waldo if you don't come and get him right away, because he's already befuddled Miss Wilson into going to Boston with him tonight, and starting out again from there the first thing in the morning. He's got Miss Wilson believing everything he says, the lies along with the common truth. Looks like she would be on her guard, knowing she's associating with a newly-rich, but she's too far gone to listen to reason. Waldo pulls out his wealth every few minutes and waves it in front of her, and the sight of that big roll of greenbacks acts on her just like chloroform would on an average being. I've done my best to—"

Dessie gripped the phone.

"Did you say Waldo has a big roll of money?" she shouted. "Greenbacks tied with a string around the middle?"

"He surely has, Mrs. Murdock. It's the biggest roll of money I've seen on a man since the Democrats took over."

Dessie, who had risen from the chair until she was almost erect, sat down, hard.

"Let him be!" she said coldly. "I don't want part or parcel of him. He had me digging in stony ground all day looking for that money in a coffee can, and it wasn't there at all. Let the schoolteacher take him. I've had my share, and more, of suffering, and now I'd be comforted to see somebody else have a goodly portion of it. Sudden wealth will show up a man's true nature every time, and I'm glad I found out the true size and shape of Waldo Murdock's nature before I wasted another single day of my life on him."

"You mean you're not going to try to stop Waldo from going away to the other end of the world with Miss Wilson?"

"No!" Dessie said emphatically. "Waldo Murdock has a free hand from now on!"

She hung up the receiver. A moment later she slumped brokenly in the chair. She called Justine several times before remembering that Justine had gone out with Carl Friend.

After that she hurried into her clothes and went back to the phone. She rang up Thornton Blanchard, her lawyer, and told him to come right away. He lived only a few miles distant, and he promised to be there within fifteen minutes.

While waiting for Thornton Blanchard, Dessie paced up and down the hallway, her face grim and determined. Her mind was made up, and she knew the sooner she acted the better she would feel.

After a few more minutes, he drove up to the house and stopped his car in the dooryard. Dessie went to the step, holding the door open for him. Thornton Blanchard hurried inside and went directly to the table in the center of the living room.

"Is there something wrong, Mrs. Murdock?" he asked anxiously.

"There is now, but it won't be much longer," she said, sitting down at the table, "not after I set things right I should have attended to twenty years ago."

Blanchard sat down and opened his briefcase, slipping out a pad of ruled yellow writing paper and a pencil. He watched Dessie's face, waiting for her to begin.

"Are you ready?" she asked.

"Yes, Mrs. Murdock," he told her, adjusting the pad on the table.

"I want a divorce," she said quickly, "and I want it in a hurry. How soon can I get it, or do I have to go find myself a better lawyer?"

Blanchard sat up.

"Joking aside, Mrs. Murdock, right after you and your husband inherited all that wealth, you want a divorce?" he asked unbelievingly.

"That's what I said."

"But why?"

"Never mind my reasons," she answered. "When I go to the store and ask for a pound of sugar, I don't have to tell the clerk my reasons for wanting it, do I?"

"No, but—"

"Then go ahead and get me my divorce."

Blanchard fingered the writing pad nervously. After several moments he shook himself, and glanced across the table at Dessie.

"Have you any grounds, Mrs. Murdock?" he inquired cautiously.

"Of course, I've got grounds. I've got all the grounds needed and a plentiful supply to spare."

"What are to be the grounds on which the suit is to be based, Mrs. Murdock?" he asked, bending over the pad and gripping the pencil tightly.

"Cussedness," she said, leaning back.

Blanchard looked up.

"That's what I said," she nodded. "Cussedness!"

"The judge that hears this suit might not—"

"I don't care what the judge thinks," she retorted. "It's my divorce, and I'll have grounds of my own choosing whether the judge likes them or not."

Blanchard tapped the pencil on the table several times, his mind deep in thought.

"As your attorney, Mrs. Murdock," he said finally, "would you mind telling me in confidence on just what grounds you do base your contention?"

"Waldo Murdock tricked me," she said angrily, relieved to have an opportunity to talk about her troubles. "He went and made as if to bury the inheritance in a coffee can behind the barn, but didn't, and then went off and stayed from home all day while I broke my back, and Justine's, too, digging in stony ground for it."

Blanchard drew the palm of his right hand slowly over his face. He leaned back after that and gazed professionally at the ceiling. He was doing his best to keep from saying, on the spur of the moment, anything of a rash nature.

"And I want alimony, too," Dessie spoke up. "I want all of it."

Blanchard sat up.

"What do you mean by all of it?"

"All the inheritance, of course," she replied.

Blanchard was silent for some time. He looked at the pad, studying the texture of the paper minutely. After a while he looked up at Dessie, fortifying himself with several deep breaths.

"It's going to be difficult, if not impossible," he said gravely. "Downright difficult, Mrs. Murdock."

"That's your job," Dessie told him. "I've worked hard for my living, too."

Blanchard expelled the breath from his lungs and took a fresh start.

"For one thing, Mrs. Murdock, we have no community property law in this state." He leaned back, rolling the pencil between the palms of his hands. "Naturally, that rules out automatically any possibility of a legal division of Waldo's wealth, whatever it may amount to. But let me put it another way. I'll review briefly the background of the whole matter. A wife is subject, more or less, to the will of the husband, all things being equal, of course. However, the marriage contract also subjects the husband to the will of the wife, placing the shoe on the other foot, so to speak. Now we arrive at the conclusion that the two members of the partnership are each and individually subject to the will of the other. But, and let me speak frankly, in our present society, it is the wife's own responsibility to devise, instate, and employ methods, means, and opportunities for enticement that will cause her spouse to desire of his own free will and accord to bestow, shall we say, a single largess, or, as the case often is, continuing largesses, upon her while united in wedlock. Now, as you no doubt realize, Mrs. Murdock, the average wife, to put it bluntly, by showering her favors upon her spouse obtains, in most instances, a bountiful

portion of his goods, chattels, and wealth, in some cases benefits that, judged by worldly standards, are far out of proportion
to the value—"

"No!" Dessie said emphatically.

Blanchard cleared his throat and bit his underlip.

"It might be best, in the long run, to let the presiding judge
set the sum you might obtain from your present husband," he
said wearily. "I'm afraid I won't be of much help in that connection. However, I can proceed with filing the divorce papers,
and the matter of alimony can be taken up in due course."

"When can I see the judge about getting the money?" Dessie
asked. "Tomorrow morning?"

"I'm afraid not," he said, shaking his head. "Your suit couldn't
possibly come up for trial until the next term of court, come
autumn."

"Come autumn!" Dessie cried.

Blanchard nodded.

"You mean wait all that time!" she cried excitedly. "Why,
Waldo Murdock will have every penny of the wealth spent
long before then. There wouldn't be anything left for me to
sue for!"

"Well," Blanchard said, shaking his head, "I don't know what
can be done, then. The terms of court are set by statute."

The side door burst open, and they both turned around to
find Waldo standing in the doorway blinking his eyes in the
bright light. After adjusting his vision, he walked into the room
and went to the vacant chair between Dessie and Blanchard.

"How be you, Thornton?" Waldo said, reaching out and
grasping Blanchard's hand. He shook it hard.

"Fair," Blanchard said uneasily. He glanced at Dessie. She
was staring at Waldo. "Fair," he said again.

Waldo seated himself.

"Thought for a while today I needed to see you about a
matter, but I changed my mind. There's no need, now."

"Well, I'm glad you handled the matter without needing any
help," Blanchard said, stumbling over the words.

"Decided not to bother handling it," Waldo said, "so I just dropped it."

"That's fine," Blanchard said, wondering.

Waldo made himself comfortable.

"Was trying to figure out a way to have a good time and keep the money, too. Figured it couldn't be done. So I decided to get shet of it."

Dessie was about to leap from her chair when Waldo reached into his pants pocket and tossed the big roll of greenbacks across the table to her. The tightly bound roll of money tumbled into her lap.

For a moment Dessie looked as if she did not know what in the world had happened. Then slowly her eyes began to bulge and she looked down into her lap. She stared at the money dazedly.

"Waldo—" she said, her speech choked.

Tears began to flow down her cheeks, and Waldo squirmed uneasily in his chair. He dropped his head, glancing up at her from beneath his eyebrows every now and then.

"Waldo—" she began again. She could not continue.

Waldo wiped his mouth with the back of his hand.

"Figured a man with no more sense than I've got ought not be allowed to possess that much wealth," he said, still looking down. "So I decided there was only one thing to do and that was to get shet of it." He glanced from Dessie to Blanchard. "It makes me feel better to be shet of it, the whole three hundred and fifty dollars of it."

Her chair falling over backward as she jumped to her feet, Dessie ran to Waldo. She dropped on her knees beside him and threw her arms around him.

"Waldo—that schoolteacher—"

"The mind was weaker than the eye," he said, glancing up at Blanchard. "The mind was weaker than the eye until she said she wanted me to give her the money to carry."

He looked down admiringly at Dessie.

"Waldo," she said haltingly. "I needed that exercise out behind the barn." She looked up into his face. "It did me a lot of good."

Blanchard pushed back his chair as quietly as possible, gathering up his pad and pencil as he backed away from the table. He had almost reached the door when he was startled to hear somebody singing in the kitchen. He stopped and listened, and by that time Dessie had heard it, too. She raised her head and listened intently. It was Justine singing at the top of her voice. She had never sung like that before, not even during the day.

Dessie got up and went to the kitchen door. She threw it open and stood back.

"Come in here, Justine," she called into the next room.

Justine walked slowly past her and went as far as the table. She stood trembling, fearing she was going to be scolded for singing in such a loud voice at that time of night.

Dessie followed her to the table.

"What did you tell me this morning about not having cause to hurry marriage with Carl Friend, Justine?" she asked her.

Justine gripped her fingers tightly.

"That's what I said this morning, Mrs. Murdock," she replied after hesitating to answer for several moments. She glanced quickly around the room at Waldo and Blanchard. "But—"

Dessie nodded.

"You can't fool me when I hear such singing as I heard a minute ago, Justine," she said. "I think it would be a good thing if you and Carl Friend went ahead right away and bought that chamber suite you were speaking to me about this morning."

She handed Justine the roll of bills and walked around the table to the chair where Waldo sat. Justine looked at the greenbacks in her hand, gripping them tightly before she could bring herself to believe they were real.

"Thank you, Mrs. Murdock!" she said, tears beginning to trickle down her cheeks. "How did you know?"

"Never mind, Justine," Dessie said quickly.

Justine began backing toward the kitchen doorway.

"That money never was intended for us in the first place," Waldo said. "We couldn't have managed it, even if we had had a smart lawyer to help."

Dessie dropped on her knees beside Waldo, throwing her arms around him again. They both turned and looked toward the door where Blanchard was standing. Without a word he turned, opened the door quickly, and stepped out into the night.

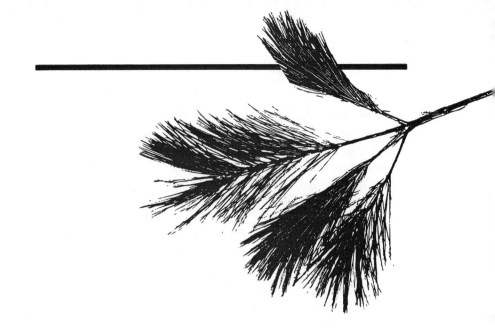

A VERY
LATE SPRING

Mary Jane knew Dave was up to some kind of
mischief, but to save her soul she could not find
out what it was. Dave had been acting queerly for
more than a month. He was nervous and restless
when he came in the house and she had a hard
time making him finish his meals. Dave said he
was just not hungry, but Mary Jane knew that
was not the real reason. He was up to some kind
of mischief.

Dave blamed it all on the weather. Here it was
the last of April and almost the first of May, he
said, and it was still winter. There should have
been a thaw three or four weeks ago, but instead

there were nineteen inches of snow and ice on the ground and the thermometer never went above the twenties. And it looked like more snow right then.

Mary Jane reminded him of the winter three years before when the spring thaw did not come until the first week in May. She said she was certain the lake ice would go out almost any day now.

Mary Jane could not see how the weather had anything to do with the way he was acting.

Instead of getting over his restlessness Dave got worse. When he came home at night, after working all day in the lumber-mill, he wanted to go out again before he finished eating his supper. There was a dance at the Grange hall every Tuesday night, and the moving-pictures every Friday night, but there was no place to go during the rest of the week. Mary Jane went to the pictures on Friday nights and to the dance whenever there was one, and the other evenings she was in the habit of staying at home and doing her lace-work. Dave wanted to go somewhere every night now.

"Why can't you sit by the fire and read the newspapers like you used to do, Dave?" she asked, with her worried frown that he had once liked so much.

"I want to go somewhere," was his answer. It was the same answer each time she asked him.

She placed supper on the table and Dave sat down in his chair.

"You act like a twelve-year-old boy, Dave," she stated accusingly. "You used to want to stay at home when I wanted to go to the dance or the pictures at the Grange hall. Now you want to go off and leave me by myself every night. What makes you so restless lately?"

"Maybe the winters are getting worse," he mumbled to himself. "I wish I lived out in California or down in Florida, where they don't have to put up with snow and ice half the whole year."

Mary Jane gave up trying to talk to Dave. Every time she asked him what made him so restless at night he always cursed the winters and said he was going where there were none. It did no good to try to talk to him. Dave did not pay any attention to her. He was always thinking about something else.

Two days later there was a four-inch snowfall. It began to snow at about eight o'clock in the morning just after Dave went to the lumber-yard. By six o'clock that night it had almost stopped, but there were four inches of it on the ground—on top of the nineteen inches already there.

Mary Jane waited all day for night to come. Not because she wanted it to come, but because she dreaded it more than anything in the world. She knew Dave would come home cursing the winters and the snow. And then before he was half-way through supper he would get up and want to go somewhere. She knew exactly what he would say about it.

Just as she knew he would do, that evening Dave stopped eating in the middle of his meal and got up from the table. She watched him go to the next room for his hat and mackinaw. Then he went to the hall and put on his heavy shoes. When he did that, she could stand it no longer. She ran to him.

"Where are you going, Dave?"

"I'm going out to walk around a while," he said nervously. "I'm going out. I'll be back after a while."

Dave went out the door and closed it behind him. She could hear the crunch of the snow under his feet while he walked down the path to the road. When he got there, the sound stopped. She knew he was walking in the deep snow and cursing about the winters.

After the dishes had been washed and the kitchen put in order, Mary Jane went to the next room and sat down in front of the fire. She had been doing a lot of thinking for the past two weeks or more, and the more she thought, the more uneasy she became. There was something that disturbed her. She could not help thinking about it because every time Dave got restless and went out it made her think about it all the more.

She had been doing a lot of thinking lately about the school-teacher the Maxwells were boarding. The teacher had been living there all winter, but Mary Jane had not seen her until about the middle of January. The girl was too young to teach school and she was too pretty to live in the village. Her name was Flora Dunn. She remembered when Dave told her. He said she was not much more than seventeen or nineteen years old. That was all he said about her, but ever since then Mary Jane had been thinking a lot. The teacher who was there the year before had been asked not to come back because she put too much coloring on her face. The Dunn girl was not like that. She was so young she was pretty without coloring.

Mary Jane suddenly sprang up and put on all her heavy clothes and went to the barn and hitched the horse to the sleigh. When that was done, she carefully took off all the harness bells. She had enough to distract her without hearing a lot of tinkling little bells on the horse. And besides, she did not want the bells on to-night, anyway. She took the bells off and laid them on the carriage seat.

She drove down the road past the Maxwell's house. Then she drove up and down in front of the house six or seven times. She stopped by a tree the last time and hitched the horse to it. After that she walked up and down the road to keep warm.

After waiting twenty minutes in the road Mary Jane saw Flora go upstairs to bed and turn out the light. In two minutes a figure came from the house and through the snow to the road. Mary Jane knew it was Flora. She was certain of that.

While she waited beside the horse and sleigh, Flora crossed the road and went down the hillside toward the cannery at the lake. Mary Jane followed her across the snow. There was no moon visible, but the clouds were so thin the moon gave enough light to enable her to follow Flora.

When Flora reached the cannery, she opened the unlocked door and went inside for a few minutes. Then she came back and stood in the doorway, looking out over the lake as though she expected somebody to come across the ice.

Mary Jane waited beside a tree. Presently she could hear a low whistle out on the lake somewhere, and almost instantly followed an answering whistle from Flora. Mary Jane waited. She knew it was Dave walking across the ice on the lake. And she knew he was coming to the cannery.

Dave came across the ice and went up the steps to the cannery door. Flora stepped back inside just as he came up, and Mary Jane could not see what they were doing. She lost no time in getting to the cannery. Then cautiously she went up the steps. The door had been closed but not locked. She opened it easily without a sound. Dave and the girl had lighted a candle and put it on the peeling-table. The light it gave was not strong enough to see everywhere inside, but she could easily distinguish Dave and the girl. They were whispering together in the corner behind the boiling-tubs.

Mary Jane slammed the door and reached for a piece of rope she saw hanging on the wall.

"Who is that?" she heard Dave's anxious voice.

Flora screamed.

Mary Jane ran across the cannery floor to the corner. She slashed Dave's face with the rope and struck Flora around her legs.

"For God's sake, Mary Jane," Dave pleaded, when he recognized her face in the candle-light. "Mary Jane, please don't do that!"

"So you got tired of waiting for the winter to pass, didn't you?" she shouted at him. "The winter made you restless, didn't it?"

She stung him again and again with the rope across his face and shoulders. She did not hit Flora again.

Flora clung to Dave's arm and would not leave him. Mary Jane got more angry when she saw Flora hanging to Dave. She drew back to strike the girl, but Dave jerked the rope from her hand.

"What's the matter with you, Mary Jane?" he shouted. "You stop trying to hurt her!"

"You shut your mouth, Dave! I'm going to teach her a lesson so she'll never bother a married man again as long as she lives!"

Dave caught her arms and held her. As soon as he touched Mary Jane she relaxed and almost fell to the floor.

"If you'll promise not to see Dave again I won't tell on you," she said to Flora. "But if you don't promise, I'll take both of you up to the house and tell the Maxwells exactly where you were and what you were doing. If I did that, you'd have to leave your school to-morrow—and anyway, you'll have better sense than to apply for this same school again next year, won't you?"

"I promise," Flora begged. "I promise I won't see him again! Please don't tell Mr. Maxwell, or anybody!"

"Well, we're going home now," Mary Jane said. "Come on."

They walked up the hill to the road. Dave walked in front, Mary Jane behind him, and Flora last. When they reached the road, Flora ran to the house without looking back.

"Come on home, Dave," Mary Jane said.

She led him to the horse and sleigh.

Neither said a word while they rode through the village. At the barn Dave unhitched the horse while Mary Jane went into the house.

When Dave came into the room, Mary Jane was looking at something in the almanac. Dave pretended not to be interested in what she was doing.

"Dave," Mary Jane said, handing him the almanac opened at the month of April, "Dave, the almanac says there's going to be a big spring thaw in northern New England beginning the 20th—and to-morrow's the 20th. Did you know that?"

"Where does it say that?" he asked anxiously, taking the almanac and holding it so the light could fall on the print. "Does it say we're going to have the spring thaw to-morrow, sure enough?"

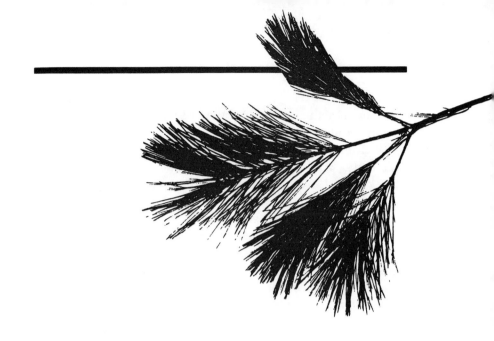

TEN THOUSAND
BLUEBERRY CRATES

No one in the village had ever heard of a wood-turning mill called the Yankee Dowel Company when the stranger asked to be directed to it. He said he was positive the plant was in the town of Liverpool, because he had a letter in his pocket with the postmark on it and the name and address of the company printed on the letter-head. There were six or seven mills of that kind in the town, the largest being over in East Liverpool and owned by Walt Brown.

"Who signed the letter you got there?" Nate Emmonds asked him.

"A man by the name of Brown," he said, looking at the letter again. "Walter J. Brown."

"Walt Brown, eh?" Nate said, glancing around at the men in the store. "Walt Brown signed the letter, and he calls himself the Yankee Dowel Company. I wonder what he could be up to now?"

A knowing wink passed from man to man around the stove.

"He used to be the Eastern Barrel Hoop Corporation," someone said, slapping his hands on his knees and having a good laugh with the other men, "but I ain't heard much about that corporation since wooden flour-barrels went out of use. Walt's been doing his durndest trying to sell me a load of barrel-hoops to stake tomato-plants with. He thinks up the queerest notions to get rid of his hoops of any man I ever saw. Who ever heard of staking tomato-plants with barrel-hoops, anyhow?"

It was several minutes before the crowd stopped laughing at Walt. He had been up to some crazy schemes in his lifetime. Only a month or two before that, he was all excited over a plan of his to make a new kind of wooden clothes-pin at his mill. Now there was something else up his sleeve. The trouble with Walt was he was always letting somebody get the better of him when it came to business deals. He got along all right as long as he stuck to his lumber business, but whenever he tried to branch out into fancy woodwork he was always licked from the start. Everybody thought he had learned his lesson after losing a lot of money in the barrel-hoop deal, and believed that he would stick to his planing and stop trying to get rich by taking up fancy dowelling. Apparently, though, he was going in for it again.

"Sure," Nate said, "I know Walt Brown. But what's your name, and what do you want to see him for?"

The man looked at Nate and then at the crowd around the stove before he said anything. He knew the men would not tell him how to find the mill until he told them his name and business.

"I'm Bullock" he said, "from over at The Falls. I buy and sell wooden products."

Androscoggin Falls was a town forty-five miles northeast of Liverpool. There were several shoe-factories there, with a dozen or more mills turning out wooden products of various kinds.

Nate slapped his hands on his knees and winked at the men around him.

"So you're a Bullock from over at The Falls, eh? I don't guess you give milk then, do you?"

Everybody in the store broke out laughing again. The man from The Falls could not keep from laughing either.

"No," he said, suddenly getting red in the face and looking angry. "No, I don't give milk, but I'm a damn hard butter when I get wild and loose."

The crowd took it all in without a sign. The men knew Nate had run up against a man every bit as sharp-witted as he was. Nate looked at Bullock very hard for a moment, but he had nothing to say to that answer.

"Come on outside," Nate told him, "and I'll show you how to find Walt Brown's mill."

When they were out in the street Nate offered him some smoking tobacco and admired his automobile. It was not long before both of them were laughing and telling each other jokes.

Bullock said finally that he was in a hurry to find the mill and get back to The Falls. Nate told him to take the upper lake road three miles to East Liverpool. Walt's mill was at the end of the lake where the State road crossed the stream.

It did not take him long to go the three miles in his car. When he reached East Liverpool he walked into the mill and found Walt operating one of the wood-turning machines. There were five or six other men working in the plant with him.

"You're Walter Brown, aren't you?" Bullock asked him.

"I'm the one," Walt said. "What do you want?"

"I'm Bullock, from over at The Falls. You sent me some prices on cider-jug-handles last week. I came over to talk business with you."

Walt brightened up immediately. He shut off the machine he was running and took Bullock to his office in the house across the street.

"That's a fairly good price you gave me on fifty gross," Bullock said. "I've got a chain store begging for some right away, so if I were to double that number could you shade the price a little?"

"Well, I guess maybe I can," Walt said. "And I guess maybe we can do business together."

Walt was very much excited over the prospect of getting a big order for wooden handles. When he had sent Bullock the quotation the week before, he had not expected it to amount to anything. Some people said his prices were too high, and that his plant was too far away from the railroad for him to get much business without offering f. o. b. shipments like the rest of the mill men. It cost a lot of money to truck twenty-seven miles to the depot.

Bullock signed the order for a hundred gross of the jug-handles and gave Walt shipping directions. He knew he would have to pay trucking costs in addition to the freight, but he had figured all that into the cost before he left The Falls. Even then he was getting the handles cheaper than ever before, and he was pleased with Walt's price. The wooden jug-handles had been costing him from fifty to seventy-five cents more a gross from the mills at The Falls.

When he was about to leave he happened to see a stack of barrel-hoops in the mill. He asked Walt if he turned out hoops too. Walt explained that it was some left-over stock he had been unable to sell because people had stopped buying flour in barrels as they used to and bought it now in sacks instead.

Bullock went in and looked the lot over. Walt watched him break one of the hoops over his knee to inspect the grain in the wood. Bullock's business was dealing in wooden products on commission, but he had not had a hoop to pass through his hands in more than three years.

"I can't do anything with barrel-hoops either, these days, but I'll tell you one thing I've never been able to get enough of."

"What's that?" Walt asked quickly.

"Blueberry crates," he said. "I can't get enough of them. I could have sold five hundred only last week to a man over in New Hampshire if I could have got my hands on some. The blueberry-crate business is better this year than it ever has been. Everybody wants crates this year to ship berries to market."

Walt thought a while about blueberry crates and walked around in circles. He had made almost everything in wooden products during his lifetime, but a blueberry crate was one thing he had never thought of. He knew he could do it, though, because his machines would turn out practically anything.

"I can make blueberry crates," he said.

"If you can make delivery of them by the end of this month I can use them," Bullock said. "I'll pay the ruling price on them at the time you make delivery, too. That's a better deal for you than setting a price beforehand, because the market will be up when the season opens. I'll take as many as you can get out in that time, too. But they'll have to be ready before the end of the month, because after that the season will be too far advanced."

Walt went to his office to get an order-blank for Bullock to sign, but when he came back to the mill Bullock had gone. Walt did not like that, because he never wanted to make up an order when it hadn't been signed for in advance. In that case he could not bring suit to collect if the man refused to take the lot. But Bullock looked all right, and he talked as if he meant to take them. In the matter of blueberry crates a signed order did not mean much anyway, because if a man decided to cancel an order all he had to do was to claim the crates were not up to standard specifications.

Walt went ahead with his plans for making the crates anyway. But first he started getting out the wooden jug-handles and had his men begin work on them right away. They would finish that job in a few days, and in the meantime they could begin getting the machines ready for the crates.

He went to the village the next morning to buy some nails with which to put the crates together. He had made a sample crate the night before, and with the weight of the nails he used he had figured out an estimate for the entire lot.

When he reached the village he went to Pat Hobb's store and told Pat he wanted some crate nails. Pat talked a while about the road money, and how it was being wasted by putting in a gravel fill by the North Schoolhouse. Walt was on the town road commission but he did not have much to say. He was in a hurry for the nails so he could get back to the mill.

Pat went over to the keg and picked it up. There were not more than ten pounds of nails in it.

"How many do you want?" he asked Walt.

"How many have you got?"

"About eight to ten pounds, maybe twelve."

"I want all of those, and I'll need a lot more besides."

"But I can't sell you all I've got, Walt. Suppose somebody else came in and said they wanted some?"

"Good God, I can't help that," Walt said. "You've got them to sell, ain't you? Well, sell them to me. I'm the one that wants to buy them."

"I couldn't do that, Walt," Pat said, putting the keg on the floor again. "I wouldn't have none left if I sold them all to you."

"Good God," said Walt, "ain't you in the selling business? What do you keep store for if it ain't to sell?"

"I know, but somebody——"

"Good God, Pat, don't make me mad. You can get some more nails, can't you? I'll want a lot more myself before I'm done buying. Why, do you know how many blueberry crates I'm going to make?"

"No," Pat said. "How many?"

"Ten thousand."

"Ten thousand blueberry crates?"

"That's what I said."

"Good God, Walt, that's a heap of blueberry crates. I never heard of a man making ten thousand of them before. What are you going to do with them?"

Walt did not know just then, himself. When he had said *ten thousand* it was done to impress Pat, so he could get all the nails he wanted, but when he began to think it over he was not sure that Bullock could take that many. It would take a lot of quart baskets of blueberries to fill that many crates, and there were other mills making crates too. But Walt knew he could never back down now. Pat would tell Nate Emmonds about it, and that would make Nate take back a lot of the things he had been saying about Walt and his wooden-products business.

"I've got an order from Bullock over at The Falls for that many. Maybe more, too."

Pat remembered Bullock's coming into the store and asking for Walt a few days before that. He would tell Nate about the big number of crates Walt was making as soon as he came into the store again.

"I'll take what nails you got there, Pat," Walt said. "And I'll be back in a few days for a lot more. I'll need a pile of nails to put all those crates together."

"All right," Pat agreed, "you can take them. But I know I ain't doing best. Somebody will be sure to come in and ask for crate nails and I won't have none at all."

"You order some right away. I'll be in again soon for two or three kegs full."

Walt went back to the mill and got to work on the crates. The wooden handles for the cider and vinegar jugs would be ready by the end of the next day. After he got them off to Bullock he could put all his men to work on the crates.

Everybody in town had heard about the large number of blueberry crates Walt was going to make, and by the middle of the following day men began coming in to ask Walt for a job helping make them. Walt took on fifteen new men and went to work. By the end of the week they were turning crates out at the rate of a thousand a day. The stack in the millyard got higher and higher, and it was not long before crates were piled twenty feet high in every available place.

The piles of crates attracted the attention of a man passing through East Liverpool in his car late Tuesday afternoon of the following week. He stopped, turned around, and drove back to the mill where Walt was. Walt was too busy to stop work.

"What kind of crates are those?" he asked Walt.

"Blueberry," Walt said without turning around.

"If you had said raspberry, I couldn't have told the difference. Raspberry crates are exactly like those. And I ought to know, because raspberry crates is my business."

"What do you want?" Walt asked him. "I can't waste time talking when I've got work to do."

"I want to buy those crates," the man said. "I had just started on a buying trip to get raspberry crates for my customers. I buy and sell wooden products on commission, and if you'll meet my offer halfway we can do business. I'll take all the crates you've got and haul them away in my own trucks starting tomorrow. You'll sell them to me, won't you?"

"Nope," Walt said, "I won't sell them to you. And those ain't raspberry crates, either—them are blueberry crates. And anyway, they are already bargained for. I'm making them on order."

Walt could not understand why the man called them raspberry crates. If he had learned the business of making crates before he jumped into it, he would have known that blueberry crates had to be made up in bundles because most of them were shipped several hundred miles down East on the coast, while raspberry crates were usually nailed together at the time they were made because they were used in this section of the State and it was cheaper and a saving of time to truck them to the fields directly from the mills. A distance of fifty miles was all that was necessary at times to change the name and use of a crate.

"This is the first time I ever saw blueberry crates put together at the mill. All the blueberry people I know want the parts shipped to them in bundles, and then they knock the crates together right in the fields where——"

"When you've been in the wooden-products business for as long a time as——"

"Then you're not going to sell me those raspberry crates even if I——"

"These blueberry crates are already bargained for. And if they was raspberry crates I wouldn't sell——"

"I've got to be going," the man said. "I can't waste my time standing here talking all day to a blundering fool."

"If you don't get going I'll have to waste some of my time looking for a piece of four-by-four to start you off with."

The man knew he could never persuade Walt to sell the crates, no matter what name he called them by, so he went back to his car and drove away. He had been dealing with mill men in that section of the State for thirty years, and he knew that whenever one of them talked as Walt did there was never anything but time and temper lost in trying to buy something from him.

Two days before the crates would be finished, Walt wrote Bullock a letter telling him when they would be ready and asking for shipping instructions.

Bullock drove over from The Falls the same day he received Walt's letter. He did not know what to do with the crates just then, because the season would be over in another week or two. But he figured that Walt would have only two or three or, at the most, five hundred crates, and he could take them to The Falls and carry them over to the next season and still make a good profit.

When he reached East Liverpool and saw the millyard he almost had a heart-attack. He had never seen so many blueberry crates in all his life, and he had been dealing in them for twenty years.

When he had first talked to Walt about making crates he had no idea Walt intended making them, at least not in such quantities, and he was certain he had not signed an order for them.

But he wanted to continue getting wooden jug-handles at the good price Walt had made him. There was no other mill in the whole State that would sell handles to him at that figure. Bullock knew if he told Walt he had not ordered the crates, Walt would be angry about it and perhaps refuse to sell him any more cider-jug handles.

Before Walt came out of the mill, Bullock had a few minutes to think about what he was going to say. He knew it would ruin him to take that many blueberry crates merely to please Walt.

Walt came out of the mill and met Bullock at his car. Bullock was sitting on the running-board looking at the crates in the millyard stacked higher than the buildings themselves.

"Well, Bullock," Walt said, shaking his hand, "they're ready. The last durn one of them. There's ten thousand waiting for you."

"Ten thousand!" Bullock gasped. "Ten thousand what?"

"Crates, man—blueberry crates."

"Ten thousand blueberry crates?"

"Sure," Walt said. "When I undertake a job I finish it. I made ten thousand of them for you, and I could get out half that many more by the end of the week if you want them. I've got fifteen extra men helping in the mill."

"Ten thousand," Bullock said again, still unable to realize that there were that many blueberry crates in the world.

"What's your shipping instructions? Where do you want them sent—over to The Falls?"

Bullock rose to his feet and supported himself against the side of his automobile.

"Good God," he said, wiping his face with the back of his hand.

"What's the matter?" Walt asked him.

"I'm afraid there's been a mistake," he said. "A pretty bad mistake, too. I guess probably I should have told you about it in the first place, because I've found that nearly every mill man in the State makes the same mistake when he undertakes to make blueberry crates. And naturally it's pretty hard on the mill man."

"What do you mean? There ain't no mistake. You said you wanted as many crates as I could make, didn't you? You said you'd take all I made. There ain't no mistake on my part."

"Yes, it's a bad mistake," Bullock said, gravely shaking his head from side to side. "You see, your business is in dowels principally, isn't it? And going back to the bottom of things, you are in the lumber business. That's your main business. All this kind of work making crates and hoops and jug handles is a sort of side-line with you. Well, that shows you're not a blueberry-crate man at all. That's why you didn't know you were making a mistake. A blueberry-crate man would never have done that."

"Done what?" Walt begged. "What's the matter with the crates I made?"

"Your crates are put together. They would have to be knocked down and bundled before they would be of any use to me. Why, man, it would cost a fortune to truck those empty crates to the depot and ship them by freight to my customers all over the State. That many empty crates would take up more space than the railroad has got boxcars to put them in. That's the mistake. You'll have to knock them down before I can use them."

"But this other man said he would haul raspberry crates away just like they stand now, if——"

"Good God, man," Bullock said, "we're talking about blue-berry crates. I didn't say anything about raspberry——"

"That's right," Walt said. "I just got mixed up in what I was saying."

Walt wished Bullock would go away and leave him alone. He felt very cheap there with Bullock, having all those crates on his hands, whatever kind they were now. But no matter how hard he tried to think his way out of the trouble he was in, he still knew the crates had been thrown back on him. If he hired the men to knock the crates down and bundle them he would lose at least two or three hundred dollars on the deal. He could not afford that. And he knew he could not force

Bullock to take them, because there was no signed contract. He remembered about the pile of barrel-hoops stacked up in the mill, too. They had been left on his hands because he nailed them together. Instead of nailing the ends together they should have been bundled and shipped flat. And now there was no market for hoops of any kind. Then his mind raced back to the crates. He wished he had asked the man who wanted to buy them for raspberry crates to leave his name and address. He could ask Bullock to put him in touch with the raspberry-crate man, because Bullock would probably know every wooden-products buyer in the State, but Walt didn't want to do that. The other man had been very angry when he left, and he would probably refuse to have anything to do with Walt after being ordered away from the mill.

"Well, I guess I'll keep them," Walt said. "I don't want to knock them down. There wouldn't be any sense in doing that."

"Suit yourself," Bullock said. "But I can't use them as they are now. They would have to be knocked down and bundled. Now, if I was in the *raspberry*-crate business I could take every one you've got. Raspberry crates——"

"These ain't raspberry crates," Walt said stiffly. "Them are blueberry crates."

Walt went back into the mill. Bullock followed him, saying something about signing an order for fifty gross of cider-jug handles that he wanted added to the first order. Walt brought him an order-blank and watched him fill it in and sign it. The moment Bullock finished writing his signature he got into his automobile and started towards The Falls as fast as he could.

When Bullock was out of sight, Walt went to the millyard and looked at the stacks of blueberry crates a while. Then he went back into the mill and looked at the barrel-hoops. He was wondering what Nate Emmonds would say about him this time.

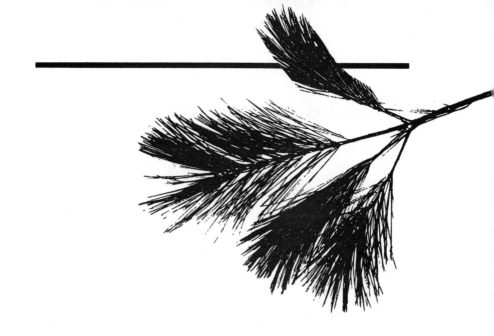

THE SICK HORSE

Benton came running around the corner of the house yelling for me to come quick. I didn't have a chance to ask him then what the trouble was, but when we got to the barn, I heard Benton saying that something was the matter with King. I had been looking for that, and I wasn't a bit surprised. If a man ever got the worst end of a bargain, I sure thought it was Benton the Friday before, when he swapped Jim Dandy for King and a durn rusty mowing machine.

All I could think of then was that maybe the best thing for the new horse was a stiff dose of medicine. I didn't have a chance to mention that to Benton until after we got inside and had opened the stall door.

Benton was blocking the door and I couldn't see the horse right away.

"Is he down yet, Benton?" I said, pushing past him.

Benton jumped aside as if somebody had jabbed him in the ribs.

"He don't have to get down for me to know he's sick, Clyde," he said. He put his hand on King's bony rump and stared at the scrawny tail. "I should have had the sense to have found out before I traded if he was taken to sick spells. But somehow I was thinking of something else—"

Benton stood back and I had a good look at King. I'd seen him in the sunlight the day the trade was made, and I never thought I'd see a worse-looking nag, but when I took a good look at him this time, I knew I'd never seen a bundle of horse-hide like that in all my life. King was standing on four legs that looked like they had been—well, to tell the whole truth, that horse looked for all the world like one of those playthings the kids make by sticking match stems into a potato.

"I reckon we should have kept Jim Dandy," Benton said, stopping short and looking at the horse. "But I had a feeling at the time—"

"He needs medicine, Benton," I said. "He needs it bad."

Jim Dandy was the finest horse we'd ever had. I guess Benton was thinking that too, because he kept glancing over to the next stall where Jim Dandy's halter was still hanging. Benton had made up his mind to swap, though, and he got a mowing machine to boot. I could tell by looking at King that he'd never last long enough to eat the hay that mower cut.

"Clyde," Benton said, "what had we better do?"

"He's real sick," I said. "He needs bracing up or something right away."

Benton didn't say anything for a while, and I looked around, and the minute I saw his face I knew what he was thinking. He was standing there looking at King and wondering what the visitors who were always dropping in to see the horses would say about that one. I'd seen ones a lot better-looking than King led off to the boneyard, and so had Benton, too.

"Better go get the castor oil, Clyde," Benton said, sitting down on the harness bench.

He was almost as sick as King was, but there was nothing I could do for him.

"Maybe we'd better wait and see if he won't get better first," I said. "That horse looks now like he might not be able to stand castor oil yet, Benton."

"Go get the castor oil like I said, anyway," Benton told me.

I went through the barn door and on into the house where the medicine was kept. When I got back, Benton had got up and gone around to the other side of King, and the horse looked just as sickly on that side as he did from any other direction. I knew that if he ever got rid of him we'd have to make a trade sight unseen.

I set the medicine on the harness bench. Right then King looked like he'd never live to stomach it.

"Give it to him, Clyde," Benton said weakly.

"Benton," I said, "I wouldn't try to force King in the shape he's in. He looks kind of white around the gills."

"Give it to him, anyway. If he won't get well, I don't want him standing around here looking like that."

Right then and there I had a feeling that the better use of the castor oil was to take it out behind the barn and pour it over the rust on the mowing machine, but there was no way to talk Benton out of giving it to King.

I went over to the harness room and got the gun and filled it with the castor oil like Benton said to. Benton did not make a move to help me. When I got back and was ready to give it to King, I motioned to Benton, and he came over and helped me get the horse's head up.

When it was all over, instead of helping me with the hay, Benton went into the house and sat down. He took a seat by the front window hoping, I guess, to be able to shy visitors away from the barn if any should stop in that afternoon.

I went on about finishing up my work and didn't have a chance to see Benton again until late in the afternoon. I had heard one car stop in front of the house, but whoever it was got headed off by Benton at the front gate and didn't get a chance to come to the barn where the sick horse was.

About five o'clock I walked around to the front of the barn and sat down to wait for Benton to come out. I knew he would be there before feeding time to look at King, and I did not want to miss seeing if the medicine had helped any. I couldn't get it out of my head all that time about trading Jim Dandy for King and the rusty mower. It was a fool trade, if there ever was one, and I couldn't figure out what had made Benton go and do it. Jim Dandy was just about the finest horse a man could hope to own. He was a good height and just about perfect in weight, and he had the finest mane and tail I ever expect to see again on a horse.

I'd always rubbed him down twice a day, and I had even got so I would rather do that than take a day off and go to town. I'd curry him and brush him until his sides were as shiny as new paint. The cold weather always ruffled up his hide, and when I started in, it would be as fuzzy as a kitten's. By the time I had finished, he looked like he'd just stepped out of the show ring with a blue ribbon. Then I'd start on his tail and mane and spend another hour working over that. I'd comb him carefully first, and then I'd begin brushing them. His mane was as silky and smooth as a young girl's hair, and those waves would come out and shine just like they had been put there with a curling iron.

But it was his tail that showed up the wavy streaks so well. His tail reached all the way down to the ground, and after you'd worked over it three quarters of an hour and stood back to let the sunshine play on it, it looked exactly like a frozen lake that had locked up with the frost when the wind was high. You can see the same thing in November before the snow falls by standing on a hilltop somewhere and looking down a mile or two away and see one of those sheets with the waves locked up in the ice. I tell you, there's not a prettier sight anywhere than that, and that's exactly how the curly waves in Jim Dandy's mane and tail looked.

I don't know how long I'd been sitting there in the sun thinking about Jim Dandy when Benton opened the house door and came down toward the barn. Just then a car drove up, but Benton was too busy thinking about something else to hear it; and two men got out and came on down toward the barn where we were.

Benton had his head down, and I couldn't motion to him till he got to the barn door, and then it was too late. Henry Trask and Fred Welch were too close to the barn by then to head off. I couldn't do a thing but just stand there and pray that they would never get inside to see King.

"Well," Benton said, "I guess we'd better go take a look."

It wasn't till then that he heard Henry and Fred behind him. Benton jumped like he was trying to get out of his skin.

"I heard you've got a new horse, Benton," Henry said. "Trying to keep it a secret? Tell Clyde to lead him out and let us get a look at him. And don't go trying to tell me he's a better horse than Jim Dandy, Benton."

Benton didn't know what to say then. He knew there was no way to get Henry and Fred away before they saw the horse. They had already got to the door, and nothing in the world could stop them then. They'd come eight miles to take a look at King.

"Henry," Benton said, "I wish you and Fred hadn't come here today."

"Why?" Fred asked. "What's the trouble, Benton? Your wife ailing or something?"

"My horse is sick," Benton said, reaching out for the side of the barn to find support. Nobody could have looked more sick than Benton did right then, but somehow both Henry and Fred failed to notice it.

"That's all right, Benton," Henry said. "You won't have to lead him out. We'll go inside and look at him in the stall."

We all walked inside and went down through the harness room and opened the door to the stall. Benton stood back. He acted like he never wanted to look at King again. Anyway, he opened the door and stepped back instead of leading the way inside as he usually did when he was proud to show the horse he owned.

"There's no horse in here, Benton," Henry said, coming back through the door. "Is this a joke or something? The stall's as empty as a Baptist church at blueberrying time."

Both me and Benton stepped to the door and looked inside. Sure enough, King wasn't there. We didn't know what to think.

"He was there right after noontime," Benton said excitedly, "because me and Clyde came in here and gave him a gunful of castor oil, didn't we, Clyde?"

"Sure as I've got legs to stand on," I said. "And he couldn't have got out, because this door has been latched all day long."

We ran inside, Benton and me. Then we saw what had happened. The side of the stall next to the areaway had been kicked down. All but the two bottom boards had been smashed to pieces.

Henry and Fred were standing behind us.

"That's the quickest I ever saw a horse get well," Benton said. "Here I've been all day trying to keep people from coming in to see King, and here he goes and gets well and kicks the side of the stall down."

Benton was all excited, thinking that King had turned out to be a fine spirited horse, after all, in spite of his looks.

"Come on," Benton said, leaping over the splintered boards. "He's back in the areaway. I know he's not out, because all the doors stay locked."

The four of us ran out into the areaway, where all the harnessing is done, but King wasn't anywhere in sight. The outside door was shut and latched just like Benton had said it was and just like I knew it was. But King wasn't in the areaway, either.

"Maybe he got into another stall or into the grain room," Henry said.

We went down toward the other end of the barn.

"He couldn't have got into another stall," Benton said, "because the rest of the stalls are on the other side of the one he was in. There's no other way for him to go, that I can see. The grain-room door is shut tight."

Just the same, to make sure, I opened it and looked around inside, but King wasn't there and hadn't been there.

It was the strangest thing I'd ever seen. I was stumped. Benton didn't know what to do next, either.

"What's that door lead into?" Henry said, walking to the door beyond the grain room.

"Shucks," Benton said, "there's no sense opening that door, because that's just a sort of privy me and Clyde use in the winter when we're working in the barn."

Henry took a couple of steps, and stopped short around the corner of the grain room.

"There's no sense in opening the door, all right," Henry said. "It's already open."

The rest of us ran down so we could see what he was talking about.

Right then—well, I don't know what anybody said after that. It was—I had to look three or four times myself before I knew what I was doing, and even then—sometimes I still can't believe what I saw. Benton—if Benton—but there's no use in trying to tell what Benton said. The whole thing—

We all finally got outside the barn someway. Benton sat down on a bench and looked off across the hills. Both Fred and Henry were laughing too much to talk sense any more. First they'd say something about Benton's new horse, and then they'd look at each other, and then they'd break out laughing all over again.

"Benton," Henry said after they had quieted down some, "it was worth your losing a horse just to know that your stock is the smartest in the country, wasn't it? I've seen horses do smart things, but this is the first time I ever saw or heard of one being smart enough to go to the privy when he took sick."

Benton got up.

"But King died in there, though," he said. "I've lost him, Henry."

"That's just it, Benton," Fred said. "Any horse that had enough sense to back in there and die on the bench proves that even when your horses are nothing to look at, they are still the smartest in the country."

Benton could not see it in that light then. He was still worried to think that the tale would hurt his reputation as a horseman. Henry and Fred left soon afterward, still laughing like I knew they would be for the next four or five days, and I didn't see much of Benton till late in the evening.

At bedtime Benton came upstairs while I was undressing to pass the night. He walked across the room and back before he said anything.

"I wouldn't have had that to happen for anything in the world, Clyde," he said. "I'd a heap rather have a horse of mine drop dead in the show ring—than that."

"I don't know, Benton," I said. "It takes a smart animal to do a thing like that. Maybe King figured that he had to make up someway for his lack of looks."

Benton came over to the table.

After a while he looked up at me. A change had come over his face.

"You're right, Clyde," he said. "It just goes to prove what I've felt ever since I was ten years old, when I started handling horses, and that is that there's no bad horses. Some of them have good looks, some have good sense, and the ones that don't have looks have the other, because all horses have some sense."

"Well, King didn't have any looks, but he sure had horse sense," I said.

Benton jumped to his feet.

— 84 —

THE SICK HORSE

"That's it, Clyde! Horse sense! I knew as well as I knew my name that that fellow I traded with thought he had stung me, and so did you and everybody else; but I could tell by watching King that day that he had what every horse worth his currycomb ought to have. By God, Clyde, King had horse sense!"

THE CORDUROY
PANTS

Two weeks after he had sold his farm on the back
road for twelve hundred dollars and the Mitch-
ells had moved in and taken possession, Bert
Fellows discovered that he had left his other pair
of corduroy pants up attic. When he had finished
hauling his furniture and clothes to his other
place on the Skowhegan road, he was sure he
had left nothing behind, but the morning that he
went to put on his best pair of pants he could not
find them anywhere. Bert thought the matter
over two or three days and decided to go around
on the back road and ask Abe Mitchell to let him
go up attic and get the corduroys. He had known

Abe all his life and he felt certain Abe would let him go into the house and look around for them.

Abe was putting a new board on the doorstep when Bert came up the road and turned into the yard. Abe glanced around but kept right on working.

Bert waited until Abe had finished planing the board before he said anything.

"How be you, Abe?" he inquired cautiously.

"Hell, I'm always well," Abe said, without looking up from the step.

Bert was getting ready to ask permission to go into the house. He waited until Abe hammered the twenty-penny into the board.

"I left a pair of corduroys in there, Abe," he stated preliminarily. "You wouldn't mind if I went up attic and got them, would you?"

Abe let the hammer drop out of his hands and fall on the step. He wiped his mouth with his handkerchief and turned around facing Bert.

"You go in my house and I'll have the law on you. I don't give a cuss if you've left fifty pair of corduroys up attic. I bought and paid for this place and the buildings on it and I don't want nobody tracking around here. When I want you to come on my land I'll invite you."

Bert scratched his head and looked up at the attic window. He began to wish he had not been so forgetful when he was moving his belongings down to his other house on the Skowhegan road.

"They won't do you no good, Abe," he said. "They are about ten sizes too big for you to wear. And they belong to me, anyway."

"I've already told you what I'm going to do with them corduroys," Abe replied, going back to work. "I've made my plans for them corduroys. I'm going to keep them, that's what I'm going to do."

THE CORDUROY PANTS

Bert turned around and walked toward the road, glancing over his shoulder at the attic window where his pants were hanging on a rafter. He stopped and looked at Abe several minutes, but Abe was busy hammering twenty-penny nails into the new step he was making and he paid no attention to Bert's sour looks. Bert went back down the road, wondering how he was going to get along without his other pair of pants.

By the time Bert reached his house he was good and mad. In the first place, he did not like the way Abe Mitchell had ordered him away from his old farm, but most of all he missed his other pair of corduroys. And by bedtime he could not sit still. He walked around the kitchen mumbling to himself and trying to think of some way by which he could get his trousers away from Abe.

"Crusty-faced Democrats never were no damn good," he mumbled to himself.

Half an hour later he was walking up the back road toward his old farm. He had waited until he knew Abe was asleep, and now he was going to get into the house and go up attic and bring out the corduroys.

Bert felt in the dark for the loose window in the barn and discovered it could be opened just as he had expected. He had had good intentions of nailing it down, for the past two or three years, and now he was glad he had left it as it was. He went through the barn and the woodshed and into the house.

Abe had gone to bed about nine o'clock, and he was asleep and snoring when Bert listened at the door. Abe's wife had been stone-deaf for the past twenty years or more.

Bert found the corduroy pants, with no trouble at all. He struck only one match up attic, and the pants were hanging on the first nail he went to. He had taken off his shoes when he climbed through the barn window and he knew his way through the house, with his eyes shut. Getting into the house and out again was just as easy as he had thought it would be. And as long as Abe snored, he was safe.

— 89 —

In another minute he was out in the barn again, putting on his shoes and holding his pants under his arm. He had put over a good joke on Abe Mitchell, all right. He went home and got into bed.

The next morning Abe Mitchell drove his car up to the front of Bert's house and got out. Bert saw him from his window and went to meet Abe at the door. He was wearing the other pair of corduroys, the pair that Abe had said he was going to keep for himself.

"I'll have you arrested for stealing my pants," Abe announced as soon as Bert opened the door, "but if you want to give them back to me now I might consider calling off the charges. It's up to you what you want to do about it."

"That's all right by me," Bert said. "When we get to court I'll show you that I'm just as big a man as you think you are. I'm not afraid of what you'll do. Go ahead and have me arrested, but if they lock you up in place of me, don't come begging me to go your bail for you."

"Well, if that's the way you think about it," Abe said, getting red in the face, "I'll go ahead with the charges. I'll swear out a warrant right now and they'll put you in the county jail before bedtime to-night."

"They'll know where to find me," Bert said, closing the door. "I generally stay pretty close to home."

Abe went out to his automobile and got inside. He started the engine, and promptly shut it off again.

"Come out here a minute, Bert," he called.

Bert studied him for several minutes through the crack in the door and then went out into the yard.

"Why don't you go swear out the warrant? What you waiting for now?"

"Well, I thought I'd tell you something, Bert. It will save you and me both a lot of time and money if you'd go to court right now and save the cost of having a man come out here to serve the warrant on you. If you'll go to court right now and let me have you arrested there, the cost won't be as much."

"You must take me for a cussed fool, Abe Mitchell," Bert said. "Do I look like a fool to pay ten dollars for a hired car to take me to county jail?"

Abe thought to himself several minutes, glancing sideways at Bert.

"I'll tell you what I'll do, Bert," he proposed. "You get in my car and I'll take you there and you won't have to pay ten dollars for a hired car."

Bert took out his pipe and tobacco. Abe waited while he thought the proposition over thoroughly. Bert could not find a match, so Abe handed him one.

"You'll do that, won't you, Bert?" he asked.

"Don't hurry me—I need plenty of time to think this over in my mind."

Abe waited, bending nervously toward Bert. The match-head crumbled off and Abe promptly gave Bert another one.

"I guess I can accommodate you that little bit, this time," he said, at length. "Wait until I lock up my house."

When Bert came back to the automobile Abe started the engine and turned around in the road toward Skowhegan. Bert sat beside him sucking his pipe. Neither of them had anything to say to each other all the time they were riding. Abe drove as fast as his old car would go, because he was in a hurry to get Bert arrested and the trial started.

When they reached the courthouse they went inside and Abe swore out the warrant and had it served on Bert. The sheriff took them into the courtroom and told Bert to wait in a seat on the first row of benches. The sheriff said they could push the case ahead and get a hearing some time that same afternoon. Abe found a seat and sat down to wait.

It was an hour before Bert's case was called to trial. Somebody read out his name and told him to stand up. Abe sat still, waiting until he was called to give his testimony.

Bert stood up while the charge was read to him. When it was over, the judge asked him if he wanted to plead guilty or not guilty.

"Not guilty," Bert said.

Abe jumped off his seat and waved his arms.

"He's lying!" he shouted at the top of his voice. "He's lying—he did steal my pants!"

"Who is that man?" the judge asked somebody.

"That's the man who swore out the warrant," the clerk said. "He's the one who claims the pants were stolen from him."

"Well, if he yells out like that again," the judge said, "I'll swear out a warrant against him for giving me a headache. And I guess somebody had better tell him there's such a thing as contempt of court. He looks like a Democrat, so I suppose he never heard of anything like that before."

The judge rapped for order and bent over towards Bert.

"Did you steal a pair of corduroy pants from this man?" he asked.

"They were *my* pants," Bert explained. "I left them in my house when I sold it to Abe Mitchell and when I asked him for them he wouldn't turn them over to me. I didn't steal them. They belonged to me all the time."

"He's lying!" Abe shouted again, jumping up and down. "He stole my pants—he's lying!"

"Ten dollars for contempt of court, whatever your name is," the judge said, aiming his gavel at Abe, "and case dismissed for lack of evidence."

Abe's face sank into his head. He looked first at the judge and then around the courtroom at the strange people.

"You're not going to make me pay ten dollars, are you?" he demanded angrily.

"No," the judge said, standing up again. "I made a mistake. I forgot that you are a Democrat. I meant to say *twenty-five dollars.*"

Bert went outside and waited at the automobile until Abe paid his fine. In a quarter of an hour Abe came out of the courthouse.

"Well, I guess I'll have to give you a ride back home," he said, getting under the steering-wheel and starting the engine. "But what I ought to do is leave you here and let you ride home in a hired car."

Bert said nothing at all. He sat down beside Abe and they drove out of town toward home.

It was almost dark when Abe stopped the car in front of Bert's house. Bert got out and slammed shut the door.

"I'm mighty much obliged for the ride," he said. "I been wanting to take a trip over Skowhegan way for a year or more. I'm glad you asked me to go along with you, Abe, but I don't see how the trip was worth twenty-five dollars to you."

Abe shoved his automobile into gear and jerked down the road toward his place. He left Bert standing beside the mailbox rubbing his hands over the legs of his corduroy pants.

"Abe Mitchell ought to have better sense than to be a Democrat," Bert said, going into his house.

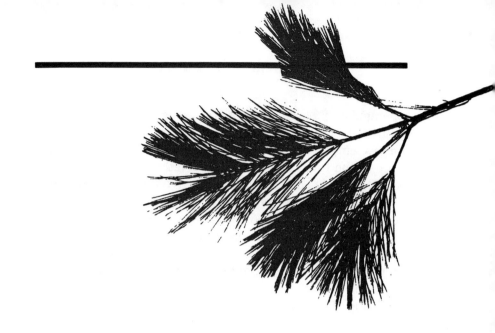

THE RUMOR

To George Williams went the distinction of being
the first to suggest making Sam Billings the new
town treasurer. The moment he made the nomi-
nation at the annual town meeting there was an
enthusiastic chorus of approval that resulted in
the first unanimous election in the history of
Androscoggin. During the last of the meeting
everybody was asking himself why no one had
ever thought of Sam Billings before.

The election of Sam to the office of town treasurer pleased everybody. He was a good business man and he was honest. Furthermore,
the summer hotel property that he owned and

operated on the east shore of Androscoggin Lake paid about a tenth of the town's total tax assessment, and during the season he gave employment to eighty or ninety people whose homes were in the town. After he was elected everybody wondered why they had been giving the office to crooks and scoundrels for the past twenty years or more when the public money could have been safe and secure with Sam Billings. The retiring treasurer was still unable to account to everybody's satisfaction for about eighteen hundred dollars of the town's money, and the one before him had allowed his books to get into such a tangled condition that it cost the town two hundred and fifty dollars to hire an accountant to make them balance.

Clyde Ballard, one of the selectmen, took George aside to talk to him when the meeting was over. Clyde ran one of the general stores in the village.

"You did the town a real service to-day," he told George. "Sam Billings is the man who should have been treasurer all the time. How did you come to think of him?"

"Well," George said, "Sam Billings was one of my dark horses. The next time we need a good selectman I'll trot another one of them out."

"George, there's nothing wrong with me as a selectman, is there?" Clyde asked anxiously.

"Well, I'm not saying there is, and I'm not saying there's not. I'm not ready to make up my mind yet. I'll wait and see if the town builds me a passable road over my way. I may want to buy me an automobile one of these days and if I do I'll want a lot of road work done between my place and the village."

Clyde nodded his head understandingly. He had heard that George Williams was kicking about his road and saying that the selectmen had better make the road commissioners take more interest in it. He shook hands with George and drove back to the village.

The summer hotel-season closed after the first week in September and the guests usually went home to Boston and New

THE RUMOR

York Tuesday or Wednesday after Labor Day. Sam Billings kept his hotel open until the first of October because there were many men who came down over the week-ends to play golf. In October he boarded up the windows and doors and took a good rest after working hard all summer. It was two or three weeks after that before he could find out what his season's profits were, because he took in a lot of money during July and August.

That autumn, for the first time in two or three decades, there was no one who spoke uneasily concerning the treasurer or the town's money. Sam Billings was known to be an honest man, and because he was a good business man everybody knew that he would keep the books accurately. All the money collected was given to Sam. The receipt of the money was promptly acknowledged, and all bills were paid when presented. It would have been almost impossible to find a complaint to make against the new treasurer.

It was not until the first real snow of the winter, which fell for three days during the first week in January, that anything was said about the new town-treasurer. Then overnight there was in general circulation the news that Sam Billings had gone to Florida.

George Williams drove to the village the same afternoon the news reached him over on the back road. He happened to be listening to a conversation on the party line when something was said about Sam Billings having gone to Florida, otherwise George might possibly have waited a week or longer before somebody came by his place and told him.

He drove his horse to the village in a hurry and went into Clyde Ballard's store. They were talking about Sam Billings when George walked in.

George threw off his heavy coat and sat down in a chair to warm his feet against the stove.

"Have you heard about it yet, George?" Clyde asked him.

"Sure I have, and God never made a bigger scoundrel than Sam Billings," he answered. "I wouldn't trust him with a half-dollar piece of my money any farther than I can toss a steer by the tail."

"I heard you was one of Sam's principal backers," one of the men said from the other side of the stove. "You shouldn't talk like that about your prime candidate, George."

Clyde came up to the stove to warm his hands and light a cigar.

"George," he said, winking at the other men around the fire, "you told me that Sam Billings was your dark-horse candidate—you must have meant to say *horse-thief.*"

Everybody shouted and clapped his knees and waited for George to say something.

"I used to swear that Sam was an honest man," George began seriously, "but I didn't think then that he would turn around and run off to Florida with all the town's money in his pants. At the next election I'm going to vote to tie the town's money around my old black cow's neck. I'd never again trust an animal that walks standing up on its hind legs."

"Well, George," Clyde said, "you ain't heard it all, about Sam yet. Can you stand a little more?"

"What else did he do?" George stood up to hear better.

"He took Jenny Russell with him. You know Jenny Russell—Arthur Russell's oldest girl. I guess he's having plenty of good times with her and the town's money down in Florida. I used to think that I had good times when I was younger but Sam Billings's got me beat a mile when it comes to anything like that."

George sat down again. He filled his pipe and struck a match.

"So he made off with a woman too, did he? Well, that's what they all do when they get their hands on some money that don't belong to them. Those two things go hand-in-hand—stolen money and women."

"He picked a good-looker while he was about it," another of the men said. "He'd have to travel a far piece to find a better-looker than Jenny Russell. And if he don't have a good time with her he ought to step aside for a younger man."

THE RUMOR

George grunted contemptuously and sucked the flame into the bowl of his pipe. He remembered the time when he had had an eye on Jenny Russell himself.

"I heard it said this morning that Sam was going to have his hotel property fired so he could collect the insurance on it," Clyde said from behind the counter where he was waiting on a customer. "If he does that, the whole town assessment will have to be changed so we will be able to collect enough tax money to keep the roads repaired and the schools running."

Nobody said anything for several minutes. George glared at each man around the stove. The raising of the tax-rate stared everybody full in the face.

Clyde came over to the stove again and stood beside it, warming his hands.

"My wife heard it said over the party line last night—" He paused and looked from face to face. Everybody in the store leaned forward to hear what Clyde was going to say. "—She heard that Sam Billings murdered one of those rich men from New York in his hotel last summer. I guess he killed him to get his money. He wouldn't stop at anything now."

"Well, I always said that Sam Billings was the biggest crook that ever lived in the town of Androscoggin," George said disgustedly. "The last time I saw Sam I thought to myself, 'Now, how in hell is Sam Billings going to keep the town's money from getting mixed up with his own?' I know now that I was right in thinking that. We ought to catch him and have him sent to the Federal prison for the rest of his life."

"He'll be a slick eel to catch," Clyde said. "Men like Sam Billings figure out their getaway months beforehand. He's probably laughing at us up here now, too. That's the way they all do."

"The Federal government knows how to catch men like Sam Billings," George said. "They can catch him if they start after him. But I don't suppose they would bother with him. We can send him to the State prison, though."

The men around the stove agreed with George. They said that if they ever got their hands on Sam they would do their best to have him sent to prison for as long a time as the law would allow.

A few days later George saw another of the selectmen and asked him about Sam Billings. George's plan of action was to get the Florida police to locate him and then have the sheriff send a deputy down to bring him back for trial. The selectman was in favor of getting Arthur Russell to have the Federal government go after Sam on the charge of taking his daughter Jenny out of the State. In that case, he explained to George, they could get Sam back without it costing the town any of its own money.

George was in favor of any plan just so long as Sam Billings was brought back and tried for stealing the money.

Later in the winter somebody told George that Sam had taken Jenny Russell and gone to Cuba with her. After that was generally known, there was nobody in the whole town who would take up for Sam or speak a word in his behalf. He had taken the town's money and made off with it. That was all there was to it.

"I never did take any stock in that Billings," George said in Clyde's store in the village. "He made so much money out of his hotel he couldn't be satisfied with what he had of his own, but had to go and take the town's money too. And if I was Arthur Russell I'd get the Federal law after him for taking Jenny off like he did. If she was my daughter and Sam Billings took her off to Florida for a good time, or wherever it was he went to, I'd get him arrested so quick it would scare the hide off his back."

"We made a big mistake when we trusted all the town's money to him," Clyde admitted. "It will take us ten years to wipe out that loss. He had almost a thousand dollars when he left."

"You were one of the fools that voted for him," George said. "It's a pity the voters ain't got more sense than they have about such things."

"If I remember correctly," Clyde retorted, "you nominated Sam Billings for town treasurer."

THE RUMOR

George went outside and unhitched his horse. He drove home without answering Clyde Ballard.

Nothing further was heard either directly or indirectly from Sam during the remainder of the winter. There were no bills that had to be paid right away though, and the town was not yet suffering because the funds were in Sam's possession.

Early that spring, when Sam usually began getting his hotel into shape for the season that opened in June, everybody in town heard one day that he was back home. Sam Billings had been seen in the village early one morning hiring a crew of carpenters and laborers. He had always made repairs on his hotel property at the same time each year.

And Jenny Russell was back home too, and everybody knew about it the same day.

There was a crew of twenty men at work around the hotel Monday morning, getting it ready for the coming season. The boards were removed from the windows and doors, and a new boathouse was being built beside the landing-float in front of the hotel. All the unemployed men in town went to the hotel and applied for jobs, because everybody knew that Sam Billings paid good wages and settled promptly every Saturday night.

Sam went about his business just as he had always done each spring. No one told him of the things that had been said about him during the past winter, and he knew nothing about the charges that Clyde Ballard and George Williams and practically everybody else in town had talked about all winter.

George went to the village the first of the week and heard that Sam was back in town for the summer. He went into Clyde's store and sat down on the counter.

"Well, I guess the town's money is safe enough," he told Clyde. "Sam Billings is back home, and I hear that Jenny Russell is too."

"I heard over the party line last night that Sam bought a big hotel down in Florida last autumn," Clyde said. "He hired Jenny Russell to go down there with him to see that the chamber-maids kept it clean and orderly. Jenny Russell is a good worker, and I guess Sam figured that she was a better supervisor than he could get anywhere else. She keeps his hotel here clean and orderly all the time."

"Sure, Jenny is a good supervisor," said George. "There's no better worker anywhere than Jenny Russell. I used to think I'd hire her for my house-keeper, and maybe marry her some day. Sure, she is a fine supervisor. Sam Billings is a good business man and he knows the kind of help he needs for his two high-class hotels."

"There's no sense in worrying about the town's money," Clyde said. "Sam Billings is an honest man."

"Sure, Sam is. There never was a more honest man alive than Sam Billings. I've known Sam all my life. The town's money is just as safe with him as it would be in my own hands. Sam Billings is an honest man, Clyde."

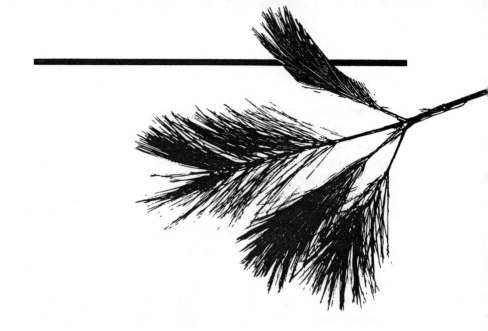

OVER THE
GREEN MOUNTAINS

Was reading a piece in the Boston paper last night about the smartest people in the whole country coming from the State of Maine. Said at the time, and I'm still here to say it: you can take your pick of any ten men in the whole Union, and I'll back one Varmonter of my own choosing against them any day. Take ten men from any of the states you can find them in, and all of them put together won't have the smartness that my lone Varmonter has got. Have lived in the State of Maine all my life, ninety-odd years of it, but I've always said that if you want some smartness you shall have to go to Varmont to get it. Varmont is where it comes from.

Now, you take the farmers. Varmont farmers is that smart they can't keep from making money while the farmers in other places is all losing money. And here is why they are so smart: not so long ago there was a Varmont farmer over here, riding around in his big auto having a good time and laughing at us farmers here because we hadn't made enough money to retire and maybe take a trip to Florida on, in even years. I asked this Varmont farmer how it was he had made so much money running a farm.

And this is what he told me: "Friend," he said, "the secret of making money out of a farm is this: Sell all you can; what you can't sell, feed to the hogs; what the hogs won't eat, eat yourself."

After he finished telling me that, he drove off laughing in his big auto to look at some more Maine farmers working and sweating in the fields because they ain't got sense enough to make money to retire on, and maybe take a winter trip to Florida, in even years.

That sporting farmer wasn't the first Varmonter I'd known, though. I used to know another one when I was a young man on the Penobscot.

This was a young fellow we called Jake Marks, one of them old-time Varmonters who used to come over here to the State of Maine driving teams of oxen before the railroads was built across the mountains. This Jake Marks was a smart one, if there ever was a Varmonter who warn't. He used to drive his oxen over here hauling freight back and forth all the time. It was a long haul in them days, when you stop to think how slow them brutes travel, and Jake had a lot of mountain to cross coming and going. I don't recall how long it took him to make one of his trips, but it was quite a time in them days when there warn't no State roads, only trails wide enough for a yoke of oxen.

Jake was a real young man at that time, I should say about twenty-five, maybe twenty-seven. He warn't married then, neither. But pretty soon he took a liking to a young and handsome filly who cooked his meals for him at the house in Bangor where he put up while he was changing cargo between trips. She was just the kind of young filly that Jake wanted, too. She used to come into the room where he sat waiting for his meal and make herself real frisky in his presence. Jake, he was tormented something awful by the way she cut up in front of him, and he used to have to get up out of his chair sometimes and walk real fast around the house three-four times to get control over himself.

But this Jake Marks was a cautious man, and he never undertook a deal until he had thought it out a lot beforehand and saw that he had everything on his side. Then, when he had thought it all through, he turned loose and went after whatever it was he wanted like a real Varmonter. All them old-time Varmonters was like that, I guess; anyway, the ones who used to drive ox freights over here to the State of Maine was, and Jake was just like all the rest of them.

This young filly of Jake's got so she pestered him about marrying of her all the time he was resting up between trips. Jake, he wanted her, all right. That was one thing he was wanting all the time he was over here. But Jake, he was taking his own good time about it, I'm telling you. He was figuring the thing out like all them Varmonters who drove ox freights did. He had to be real certain that everything was on his side before he made any signs. He took the rest of the season for figuring the thing out, and he didn't make motions of a move toward the young filly that year at all.

The next spring when the frost had thawed out of the ground and when he could make his first trip of the year over the mountains, Jake he called at the house where this young filly stayed and told her to get ready to be married to him when he got back to Bangor on his next trip. That suited the young filly first-rate. She had been uneasy all winter about Jake, taking too much at heart all the gossip that was talked about them Varmont ox freighters. But when Jake told her to get ready for marrying, she knew he would keep his promise right down to the last letter and come and marry her like he said he would.

So, Jake he went back to Varmont with his freight, promising to be ready to marry the young filly the same day he got back to Bangor on his next trip.

And just as he promised, Jake came back to get married to the young filly. He went straight to the house where she stayed, and there she was all waiting for him. Jake told her to get ready right away for the marriage, and then he went out to find a preacher somewhere. When he got back to the house with the preacher, he called her down to the room where all the guests had gathered to see the ceremony performed.

The minute she stepped into the room where Jake and the rest of the people was, Jake took one look at the young filly and told her to go back upstairs to her room and take off her dress. Well, that was all right and proper, because in those days there was a law in the State of Maine to the effect that a man could make what was called a shift-marriage. That was to say, the man could make the woman take off the dress she was wearing while the ceremony was being performed, and in that case he could not be held legally responsible for her past debts and would not have to pay them for her if he didn't have a mind to. Well, Jake he had heard all about this shift-law in Maine, and he was taking full advantage of its benefits. That was what he had been figuring out all the time he was driving them slow-footed oxen back and forth between Bangor and Varmont. Jake, he warn't no man's fool. Jake, he was a Varmonter.

After a while Jake's young filly came downstairs dressed according to this here shift-law. She had on what women wore under their dresses in those days, and that was all she had on. But Jake, he warn't satisfied, not completely. He told her to go back upstairs and take off everything she had on. Jake, he was a hardheaded ox freighter from Varmont, all right. He had figured all this out while he was driving them slow-footed oxen back and forth across the mountains.

In a little while his young filly came into the room again where Jake and the preacher and all the guests was, and she didn't have nothing on, except that she had a bedsheet wrapped around her, which was a good thing, I tell you. She was a handsome-looking filly if there ever was one.

They all got ready again for the ceremony, the preacher telling them where to stand and what to say to the questions he was getting ready to ask them. Then, just when they was beginning to get married, Jake he told his young filly to drop the bedsheet on the floor. Now, Jake he warn't taking no chances over here in the State of Maine. That shift-law said that if a woman was married without her dress on, her husband couldn't be held liable for her past debts, and Jake he figured that if the young filly didn't have nothing at all on her, there wouldn't be a chance in the whole world for to dun him for what she might owe, while if she had clothes on that he didn't know the true and legal names of, a storekeeper might try to say her underclothes was her overdress. Jake, he was thinking that he might by chance get cheated out of his rights to the full benefits of the shift-law if he didn't take care, and Jake he warn't after taking no chances whatsoever over here in the State of Maine when he was so far away from Varmont. He was as cautious where he sat his foot as the next ox freighter from Varmont.

"Drop the bedsheet on the floor," Jake he told the young filly again.

The young filly was getting ready to turn loose the bedsheet and let it drop on the floor like Jake told her to do, when the preacher he grabbed the bedsheet and held to it tight around her so she wouldn't show none of her naked self to him and Jake and the rest of the people in the house.

"No! No! No!" he yelled, getting red in the face and shaking his head at Jake. "That won't do, my man—that won't do at all! That would be indecent here before all of us! That can't be done! I'll never allow it!"

But the preacher he didn't know Jake Marks. Jake was one of them Varmont ox freighters, and he was as hardheaded about what he wanted as the next one to come along. Jake, he told the young filly again to drop the bedsheet on the floor, and to drop it quick if she wanted to get married.

The handsome young filly was getting ready to let go of it like Jake said to, because she was that crazy about Jake she would have stood on her head right then and there if Jake had told her to do it, but just when she was getting ready to let go of it, the preacher he grabbed the bedsheet again and held it fast with both hands.

The preacher started in trying to argue with Jake about it being indecent for the handsome young filly to stand there naked while she was being married, but Jake he had his head set on getting the full benefits of the shift-law and he wouldn't give in an inch.

Then the preacher said he warn't going to perform the ceremony if that was what Jake was set on doing, and Jake he told the preacher he warn't going to get married at all without the bedsheet being dropped on the floor so that none of the cloth was touching the young filly.

Everybody got excited when Jake said that, and the people talked back and forth for an hour or more, arguing first on Jake's side, because they knew the law on the books, and then on the preacher's side, because they realized how it might upset the preacher if the handsome young filly stood there naked like Jake was set on having her do. The young filly didn't care which way the ceremony was done, just so long as Jake married her. She was willing to drop the bedsheet for Jake the minute the preacher let her. She was all excited about getting married, just like Jake had been all the time.

After a while the preacher gave in to Jake just a little. He saw what a fool he was, trying to argue with a Varmont ox freighter.

"If she'll go inside the closet and shut the door so nobody can see her nakedness, I'll perform the ceremony," the preacher told Jake.

"That's all right by me," Jake said, "but I'll be compelled to have some witnesses on my side in case anybody tries to dispute me about us being married under the shift-law or not."

They finally settled that part when the preacher agreed to allow two of the older women to go in the closet with the young filly, just to make sure that everything was done in a legal manner. The preacher he didn't like to have Jake going in a closet with the naked filly, but he was pretty well worn out by that time after arguing for nearly two hours with a Varmont ox freighter, and he said he would have to allow Jake to go in the closet, too.

Jake went in the closet where the filly and the two older women were.

"Now, you just look once, Jake," the preacher said, shaking his head back and forth, "and then you shut your eyes and keep them shut."

Jake was in the closet saying something to the young filly, but nobody in the room could hear what it was. The preacher he reached over and made a bit of a crack in the door while he was marrying them so he could hear their answers to the questions. And all that time Jake he was in there striking matches to make sure that the young filly was not putting the bedsheet on again, and to be certain that he was getting the full benefits of the shift-law.

When it was all done, the preacher he took the money Jake handed him and went off home without waiting to see what shape the young and handsome filly was in when the closet door was opened. When they came out into the room, the bedsheet was all twisted up into a knot; Jake handed it to her, and she didn't lose no time in getting upstairs where her clothes were. Jake he had told her to hurry and get dressed, because he wanted to get started with his ox freight back to Varmont.

They started home to Varmont right away, the handsome young filly all dressed up in her wedding clothes and sitting on top of the freight cargo while Jake he walked along beside the wagon bellowing at the oxen.

When Jake came back to Bangor on his next trip, a storekeeper tried to present him a bill for a hundred and forty dollars. The storekeeper told Jake that the young filly had bought a lot of dresses and things just before she got married, and he wanted to know if Jake had married her under the shift-law.

Jake just laughed a little, and started unloading his cargo.

"Well, was you married that way, or the other way?" the storekeeper asked him.

"You tell me this first," Jake said, "and then I'll answer your question. Does the State of Maine have a shift-law on the books?"

"Well, yes; but the shift-law says that the woman has to—"

"Never mind about explaining it to me," Jake said. "If the shift-law is on the statute books, then that's the law I married her with."

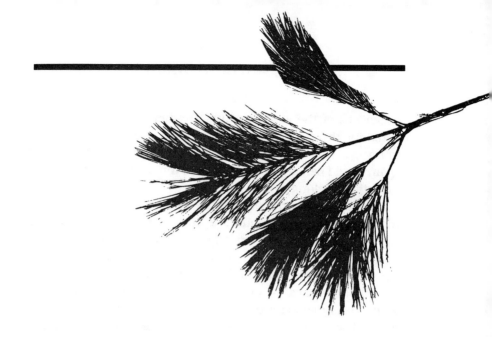

COUNTRY FULL
OF SWEDES

There I was, standing in the middle of the chamber, trembling like I was coming down with the flu, and still not knowing what God-awful something had happened. In all my days in the Back Kingdom, I never heard such noises so early in the forenoon.

It was about half an hour after sunrise, and a gun went off like a cofferdam breaking up under ice at twenty below, and I'd swear it sounded like it wasn't any farther away than my feet are from my head. That gun shot off, pitching me six-seven inches off the bed, and, before I could come down out of the air, there was another roar like somebody coughing through a megaphone, with a two-weeks cold, right in my ear. God-helping, I hope I never get waked up like that again until I can get myself home to the Back Kingdom where I rightfully belong to stay.

I must have stood there ten-fifteen minutes shivering in my nightshirt, my heart pounding inside of me like a ramrod working on a plugged-up bore, and listening for that gun again, if it was going to shoot some more. A man never knows what's going to happen next in the State of Maine; that's why I wish sometimes I'd never left the Back Kingdom to begin with. I was making sixty a month, with the best of bed and board, back there in the intervale; but like a God-damn fool I had to jerk loose and came down here near the Bay. I'm going back where I came from, God-helping; I've never had a purely calm and peaceful day since I got here three-four years ago. This is the damnedest country for the unexpected raising of all kinds of unlooked-for hell a man is apt to run across in a lifetime of traveling. If a man's born and raised in the Back Kingdom, he ought to stay there where he belongs; that's what I'd done if I'd had the sense to stay out of this down-country near the Bay, where you don't ever know, God-helping, what's going to happen next, where, or when.

But there I was, standing in the middle of the upstairs chamber, shaking like a ragweed in an August windstorm, and not knowing what minute, what Swedes do, with all their yelling and shouting and shooting off guns. Finns are quiet about their hell-raising. The Portuguese are quiet, too; you see them tramping around, minding their own business, and working hard on a river dam or something, but you never hear them shouting and yelling and shooting off guns at five-six of a Sunday morning. There's no known likeness to the noise that a houseful of Swedes can make when they get to yelling and shouting at one another early in the forenoon.

I was standing there all that time, looking out the window at the Swedes across the road, when Jim came into the kitchen with an armful of wood and threw it into the wood box behind the range.

"Good God, Stan," Jim said, "the Swedes are everywhere you can look outdoors. They're not going to get that armful of wood, anyway, though."

Mrs. Frost came to the door and stood looking like she didn't know it was her business to cook breakfast for Jim and me. I made a fire in the range and put on a pan of water to boil for the coffee. Jim kept running to the window to look out, and there wasn't much use in expecting Mrs. Frost to start cooking unless somebody set her to it, in the shape she was in, with all the Swedes around the place. She was so upset, it was a down-right pity to look at her. But Jim and me had to eat, and I went and took her by the arm and brought her to the range and left her standing there so close she would get burned if she didn't stir around and make breakfast.

"Good God, Stan," Jim said, "those Swedes are into every-thing. They're in the barn, and in the pasture running the cows, and I don't know what else they've been into since I looked last. They'll take the tools and the horses and cows, and the cedar posts, too, if we don't get out there and put every-thing under lock and key."

"Now, hold on, Jim," I said, looking out the window. "Them you see are little Swedes out there, and they're not going to make off with anything of yours and Mrs. Frost's. The big Swedes are busy carrying in furniture and household goods. Those Swedes aren't going to tamper with anything of yours and Mrs. Frost's. They're people just like us. They don't go around steal-ing everything in sight. Now, let's just sit here by the window and watch them while Mrs. Frost is getting breakfast ready."

"Good God, Stan, they're Swedes," Jim said, "and they're moving into the house across the road. I've got to put every-thing under lock and key before—"

"Hold on, Jim," I told him. "It's their house they're moving into. God-helping, they're not moving into your and Jim's house, are they, Mrs. Frost?"

"Jim," Mrs. Frost said, shaking her finger at him and looking at me wild-eyed and sort of flustered-like, "Jim, don't you sit there and let Stanley stop you from saving the stock and tools. Stanley doesn't know the Swedes like we do. Stanley came down here from the Back Kingdom, and he doesn't know anything about Swedes."

Mrs. Frost was partly right, because I've never seen the things in my whole life that I've seen down here near the Bay; but there wasn't any sense in Americans like Jim and Mrs. Frost being scared of Swedes. I've seen enough Finns and Portuguese in my time in the Back Kingdom, up in the intervale, to know that Americans are no different from the others.

"Now, you hold on a while, Jim," I said. "Swedes are no different than Finns. Finns don't go around stealing another man's stock and tools. Up in the Back Kingdom the Finns are the finest kind of neighbors."

"That may be so up in the Back Kingdom, Stan," Jim said, "but Swedes down here near the Bay are nothing like anything that's ever been before or since. Those Swedes over there across the road work in a pulp mill over to Waterville three-four years, and when they've got enough money saved up, or when they lose it all, as the case may be, they all move back here to East Joloppi on this farm of theirs for two-three years at a time. That's what they do. And they've been doing it for the past thirty-forty years, ever since I can remember, and they haven't changed none in all that time. I can recall the first time they came to East Joloppi; they built that house across the road then, and if you've ever seen a sight like Swedes building a house in a hurry, you haven't got much else to live for. Why! Stan, those Swedes built that house in four-five days—just like that! I've never seen the equal of it. Of course now, Stan, it's the damnedest-looking house a man ever saw, because it's not a farmhouse, and it's not a city house, and it's no kind of a house an American would erect. Why! Those Swedes threw that house together in four-five days—just like that! But whoever saw a house like that before, with three stories to it, and only six rooms in the whole building! And painted yellow, too; Good God, Stan, white is the only color to paint a house, and those Swedes went and painted it yellow. Then on top of that, they went and painted the barn red. And of all of the shouting and yelling, at all times of the day and night, a man never saw or heard before. Those Swedes acted like they were purely crazy for the whole of four-five days, and they were, and they still are. But what gets me is the painting of it yellow, and the making of it three stories high, with only six rooms in the whole building. Nobody but Swedes would go and do a thing like that; an American would have built a farmhouse, here in the country, resting square on the ground, with one story, maybe a story and a half, and then painted it lead-white. But Good God, Stan, those fool Swedes had to put up three stories, to hold six rooms, and then went and painted the building yellow."

"Swedes are a little queer, sometimes," I said. "But Finns and Portuguese are too, Jim. And Americans sometimes—"

"A little queer!" Jim said. "Why! Good God, Stan, the Swedes are the queerest people on the earth, if that's the right word for them. You don't know Swedes, Stan. This is the first time you've ever seen those Swedes across the road, and that's why you don't know what they're like after being shut up in a pulpwood mill over to Waterville for four-five years. They're purely wild, I tell you, Stan. They don't stop for anything they set their heads on. If you was to walk out there now and tell them to move their autos and trucks off of the town road so the travelers could get past without having to drive around through the brush, they'd tear you apart, they're that wild, after being shut up in the pulp mill over to Waterville these three-four, maybe four-five, years."

"Finns get that way, too," I tried to tell Jim. "After Finns have been shut up in a woods camp all winter, they make a lot of noise when they get out. Everybody who has to stay close to the job for three-four years likes to act free when he gets out from under the job. Now, Jim, you take the Portuguese—"

"Don't you sit there, Jim, and let Stanley keep you from putting the tools away," Mrs. Frost said. "Stanley doesn't know the Swedes like we do. He's lived up in the Back Kingdom most of his life, tucked away in the intervale, and he's never seen Swedes—"

"Good God, Stan," Jim said, standing up, he was that nervous and upset, "the Swedes are overrunning the whole country. I'll bet there are more Swedes in the town of East Joloppi than there are in the rest of the country. Everybody knows there's more Swedes in the State of Maine than there are in the old country. Why! Jim, they take to this state like potato bugs take to—"

"Don't you sit there and let Stanley keep you back, Jim," Mrs. Frost put in again. "Stanley doesn't know the Swedes like we do. Stanley's lived up there in the Back Kingdom most of his life."

Just then one of the big Swedes started yelling at some of the little Swedes and women Swedes. I'll swear, those big Swedes sounded like a pastureful of hoarse bulls, near the end of May, mad about the black flies. God-helping, they yelled like they were fixing to kill all the little Swedes and women Swedes they could get their hands on. It didn't amount to anything, though; because the little Swedes and the women Swedes yelled right back at them just like they had been big Swedes too. The little Swedes and women Swedes couldn't yell hoarse bull bass, but it was close enough to it to make a man who's lived most of his life up in the Back Kingdom, in the intervale, think that the whole town of East Joloppi was full of big Swedes.

Jim was all for getting out after the tools and stock right away, but I pulled him back to the table. I wasn't going to let Jim and Mrs. Frost set me to doing tasks and chores before breakfast and the regular time. Forty dollars a month isn't much to pay a man for ten-eleven hours' work a day, including Sundays, when the stock has to be attended to like any other day, and I set myself that I wasn't going to work twelve-thirteen hours a day by them, even if I was practically one of the Frosts myself, except in name, by that time.

"Now, hold on awhile, Jim," I said. "Let's just sit here by the window and watch them carry their furniture and household goods inside while Mrs. Frost's getting the cooking ready to eat. If they start taking off any of you and Mrs. Frost's things, we can see them just as good from here by the window as we could out there in the yard and road."

"Now, Jim, I'm telling you," Mrs. Frost said, shaking all over, and not even trying to cook us a meal, "don't you sit there and let Stanley keep you from saving the stock and tools. Stanley doesn't know the Swedes like we do. He thinks they're like everybody else."

Jim wasn't for staying in the house when all of his tools were lying around in the yard, and while his cows were in the pasture unprotected, but he saw how it would be better to wait where we could hurry up Mrs. Frost with the cooking, if we were ever going to eat breakfast that forenoon. She was so excited and nervous about the Swedes moving back to East Joloppi from the pulp mill in Waterville that she hadn't got the beans and brown bread fully heated from the night before, and we had to sit and eat them cold.

We were sitting there by the window eating the cold beans and brown bread, and watching the Swedes, when two of the little Swedes started running across Jim and Mrs. Frost's lawn. They were chasing one of their big yellow tomcats they had brought with them from Waterville. The yellow tom was as large as an eight-months collie puppy, and he ran like he was on fire and didn't know how to put it out. His great big bushy tail stuck straight up in the air behind him, like a flag, and he was leaping over the lawn like a devilish calf, newborn.

Jim and Mrs. Frost saw the little Swedes and the big yellow tomcat at the same time I did.

"Good God," Jim shouted, raising himself part out of the chair. "Here they come now!"

"Hold on now, Jim," I said, pulling him back to the table. "They're only chasing one of their tomcats. They're not after taking anything that belongs to you and Mrs. Frost. Let's just sit here and finish eating the beans, and watch them out the window."

"My crown in heaven!" Mrs. Frost cried out, running to the window and looking through. "Those Swedes are going to kill every plant on the place. They'll dig up all the bulbs and pull up all the vines in the flower bed."

"Now you just sit and calm yourself, Mrs. Frost," I told her. "Those little Swedes are just chasing a tomcat. They're not after doing hurt to your flowers."

The big Swedes were unloading the autos and trucks and carrying the furniture and household goods into their three-story yellow clapboarded house. None of them was paying any attention to the little Swedes chasing the yellow tom over Jim and Mrs. Frost's lawn.

Just then the kitchen door burst open, and the two little Swedes stood there looking at us, panting and blowing their heads off.

Mrs. Frost took one look at them, and then she let out a yell, but the kids didn't notice her at all.

"Hey," one of them shouted, "come out here and help us get the cat. He climbed up in one of your trees."

By that time, Mrs. Frost was all for slamming the door in their faces, but I pushed in front of her and went out into the yard with them. Jim came right behind me, after he had finished calming Mrs. Frost, and telling her we wouldn't let the Swedes come and carry out her furniture and household goods.

The yellow tom was all the way up in one of Jim's young maple shade trees. The maple wasn't strong enough to support even the smallest of the little Swedes, if he should take it into his head to climb to the top after the cat, and neither Jim nor me was hurting ourselves trying to think of a way to get the feline down. We were all for letting the cat stay where he was, till he got ready to come down of his own free will, but the little Swedes couldn't wait for anything. They wanted the tom right away, then and there, and no wasting of time in getting him.

"You boys go home and wait for the cat to come down," Jim told them. "There's no way to make him come down now, till he gets ready to come down of his own mind."

But no, those two boys were little Swedes. They weren't thinking of going back home till they got the yellow tom down from the maple. One of them ran to the tree, before Jim or me could head him off, and started shinnying up it like a popeyed squirrel. In no time, it seemed to me like, he was up amongst the limbs, jumping around up there from one limb to another like he had been brought up in just such a tree.

"Good God, Stan," Jim said, "can't you keep them out of the trees?"

There was no answer for that, and Jim knew there wasn't. There's no way of stopping a Swede from doing what he has set his head on doing.

The boy got almost to the top branch, where the yellow tom was clinging and spitting, when the tree began to bend towards the house. I knew what was coming, if something wasn't done about it pretty quick, and so did Jim. Jim saw his young maple shade tree begin to bend, and he almost had a fit looking at it. He ran to the lumber stack and came back dragging two lengths of two-by-fours. He got them set up against the tree before it had time to do any splitting, and then we stood there, like two damn fools, shoring up the tree and yelling at the little Swede to come down out of there before we broke his neck for being up in it.

The big Swedes across the road heard the fuss we were making, and they came running out of that three-story, six-room house like it had been on fire inside.

"Good God, Stan," Jim shouted at me, "here comes the Swedes!"

"Don't turn and run off, Jim," I cautioned him, yanking him back by his coattail. "They're not wild beasts; we're not scared of them. Hold on where you are, Jim."

I could see Mrs. Frost's head almost breaking through the window glass in the kitchen. She was all for coming out and driving the Swedes off her lawn and out of her flowers, but she was too scared to unlock the kitchen door and open it.

Jim was getting ready to run again, when he saw the Swedes coming towards us like a nest of yellow-headed bumblebees, but I wasn't scared of them, and I held on to Jim's coattail and told him I wasn't. Jim and me were shoring up the young maple, and I knew if one of us let go, the tree would bend to the ground right away and split wide open right up the middle. There was no sense in ruining a young maple shade tree like that, and I told Jim there wasn't.

"Hey," one of the big Swedes shouted at the little Swede up in the top of the maple, "come down out of that tree and go home to your mother."

"Aw, to hell with the Old Lady," the little Swede shouted down. "I'm getting the cat by the tail."

The big Swede looked at Jim and me. Jim was almost ready to run again by that time, but I wasn't, and I held him and told him I wasn't. There was no sense in letting the Swedes scare the daylights out of us.

"What in hell can you do with kids when they get that age?" he asked Jim and me.

Jim was all for telling him to make the boy come down out of the maple before it bent over and split wide open, but I knew there was no sense in trying to make him come down out of there until he got good and ready to come, or else got the yellow tom by the tail.

Just then another big Swede came running out of that three-story, six-room house across the road, holding a double-bladed ax out in front of him, like it was a red-hot poker, and yelling for all he was worth at the other Swedes.

"Good God, Stan," Jim said, "don't let those Swedes cut down my young maple!"

I had lots better sense than to try to make the Swedes stop doing what they had set their heads on doing. A man would be purely a fool to try to stop it from raining from above when it got ready to, even if he was trying to get his corn crop planted.

I looked around again, and there was Mrs. Frost all but popping through the window glass. I could see what she was thinking, but I couldn't hear a word she was saying. It was good and plenty though, whatever it was.

"Come down out of that tree!" the Swede yelled at the boy up in Jim's maple.

Instead of starting to climb down, the little Swede reached up for the big yellow tomcat's tail. The tom reached out a big fat paw and harried the boy five-six times, just like that, quicker than the eye could follow. The kid let out a yell and a shout that must have been heard all the way to the other side of town, sounding like a whole houseful of Swedes up in the maple.

The big Swede covered the distance to the tree in one stride, pushing everything behind him.

"Good God, Stan," Jim shouted at me, "we've got to do something!"

There wasn't anything a man could do, unless he was either a Swede himself, or a man of prayer. Americans like Jim and me had no business getting in a Swede's way, especially when he was swinging a big double-bladed ax, and he just out of a pulp mill after being shut up making paper four-five years.

The big Swede grabbed the ax and let go at the trunk of the maple with it. There was no stopping him then, because he had the ax going, and it was whipping around his shoulders like a cow's tail in a swarm of black flies. The little maple shook all over every time the ax blade struck it, like wind blowing a cornstalk, and then it began to bend on the other side from Jim and me where we were shoring it up with the two-by-fours. Chips as big as dinner plates were flying across the lawn and pelting the house like a gang of boys stoning telephone insulators. One of those big dinner-plate chips crashed through the window where Mrs. Frost was, about that time. Both Jim and me thought at first she had fallen through the window, but when we looked again, we could see that she was still on the inside, and madder than ever at the Swedes.

The two-by-fours weren't any good any longer, because it was too late to get to the other side of the maple in time to keep it from bending in that direction. The Swede with the double-bladed ax took one more swing, and the tree began to bend towards the ground.

The tree came down, the little Swede came down, and the big yellow tom came down on top of everything, holding for all he was worth to the top of the little Swede's head. Long before the tree and the boy struck the ground, the big yellow tom had sprung what looked like thirty feet, and landed in the middle of Mrs. Frost's flowers and bulbs. The little Swede let out a yell and a whoop when he hit the ground that brought out six-seven more Swedes from that three-story, six-room house, piling out into the road like it was the first time they had ever heard a kid bawl. The women Swedes and the little Swedes and the big Swedes piled out on Jim and Mrs. Frost's front lawn like they had been dropped out of a dump truck and didn't know which was straight up from straight down.

I thought Mrs. Frost was going to have a fit right then and there in the kitchen window. When she saw that swarm of Swedes coming across her lawn, and the big yellow tomcat in her flower bed among the tender plants and bulbs, digging up the things she had planted, and the Swedes with their No. 12 heels squashing the green shoots she had been nursing along—well, I guess she just sort of caved in, and fell out of sight for the time being. I didn't have time to run to see what was wrong with her, because Jim and me had to tear out behind the tom and the Swedes to try to save as much as we could.

"Good God, Stan," Jim shouted at me, "go run in the house and ring up all the neighbors on the line, and tell them to hurry over here and help us before the Swedes wreck my farm and buildings. There's no telling what they'll do next. They'll be setting fire to the house and barn the next thing, maybe. Hurry, Stan!"

I didn't have time to waste talking to the neighbors on the telephone line. I was right behind Jim and the Swedes to see what they were going to do next.

"I pay you good pay, Stan," Jim said, "and I want my money's worth. Now, you go ring up the neighbors and tell them to hurry."

The big yellow tom made one more spring when he hit the flower bed, and that leap landed him over the stone wall. He struck out for the deep woods with every Swede on the place behind him. When Jim and me got to the stone wall, I pulled up short and held Jim back.

"Well, Jim," I said, "if you want me to, I'll go down in the woods and raise hell with every Swede on the place for cutting down your young maple and tearing up Mrs. Frost's flower bed."

We turned around and there was Mrs. Frost, right behind us. There was no knowing how she got there so quick after the Swedes had left for the woods.

"My crown in heaven," Mrs. Frost said, running up to Jim and holding on to him. "Jim, don't let Stanley make the Swedes mad. This is the only place we have got to live in, and they'll be here a year now this time, maybe two-three, if the hard times don't get better soon."

"That's right, Stan," he said. "You don't know the Swedes like we do. You would have to be a Swede yourself to know what to tell them. Don't go over there doing anything like that."

"God-helping, Jim," I said, "you and Mrs. Frost ain't scared of the Swedes, are you?"

"Good God, no," he said, his eyes popping out; "but don't go making them mad."

THE DREAM

For six or seven years Harry had been telling me about a dream. I thought nothing of it, because nearly everyone has dreams; some of them are pleasant, others very disagreeable, but, otherwise, I could never see anything in a dream to become serious about. Each time I dreamed I remembered what happened in the dream, for a day or two, and afterwards never thought of it again. But Harry had been having the same dream regularly each month all that time. Exactly the same thing happened on each occasion, the time and place were invariably the same; and the two people had not changed in dress or appearance since the beginning. Harry was one of them; the other was a young girl. A thing like that was more than merely unfortunate; it must have been similar to the forced viewing of a motion-picture play seventy-five or a hundred times. I could imagine nothing more monotonous than that.

Harry, while he was at home the winter before, had consulted a well-known psychiatrist. The man had a reputation for correcting and curing practically every case of minor mental disorder he had undertaken, and Harry felt certain that if there was anything wrong with him the psychiatrist could help him. He went, however, to see him only once. Harry explained that the dream was recurrent each month, and the full events of it, but the psychiatrist said there wasn't anything to it. He said it was all utterly silly. He told Harry to forget it.

Probably that was his method of curing Harry. But, anyway, Harry said he lost all confidence in him after that, and he never went back again. His reason for doubting the ability of the psychiatrist to help him was that the man had said something about the impossibility of a dream's occurring more than once. But Harry's dream was recurrent. It came back again the following month, the next, and the next.

It was late June when I saw Harry the first time that summer, and he had just had his monthly dream. He told me all about it again. It was precisely the same thing he had told me the year before.

We were at the boathouse and Harry was putting a new coat of green paint on his canoe. While he was retelling the dream I was sitting against a tree. As he neared the close of the dream his paintbrush moved faster and faster, and when he reached the end the brush was moving so swiftly he could not keep enough paint in the bristles to coat the canvas.

"You finish it for me," he said, his eyes ablaze and his hands jerking nervously. "There isn't much more to paint, anyway."

I took the brush from him, and before I could reach for the paint-bucket he had disappeared in the woods behind the boathouse. I did not see him again that day.

THE DREAM

Harry's condition worried me more then than it had since he first began dreaming. It seemed to me that there must be something that could be done to help him, and perhaps cure him completely. I did not believe for a moment, however, that he would become insane. Neither did Harry. He had always been normal, and as far as I could see he was still normal. We both looked upon the dream as something temporary that would pass away at any moment.

We had known each other for ten years. Each summer we came up to Maine with our families and stayed through the season. Our camps were on the same lake, and we saw each other almost every day. We went on fishing-trips together, and we went swimming two or three times a day. Once a week we went somewhere to a dance and, more frequently, over to the village to the movies. Whenever we talked about the dream Harry always said it was as bad as ever. He said the fact that he continued having the recurrent dream was what was bad; the dream itself, however, was very pleasant.

The intensity of the dream was as memorable as the events of it. Nothing really happened, he said; it was the feeling and life-like reality that caused him so much worry. He had told me about it so many times I believed I knew how he felt. Each time, he was walking along a lonely road through a forest in northeastern Maine. The moon was out, but a thin veil of grayish clouds darkened everything and left the road and forest in a dull glow like the soft light of a shaded lamp. After he had walked a mile and a half along the road he came to a bridge over a stream. It was a timber bridge, about four and a half feet wide. He had not heard a sound or seen a single living thing until he reached the bridge. But the moment he put his foot on the bridge he heard someone call his name very softly. He looked up, and in front of him, in the centre of the gravel road, was a young girl. She was about eighteen. She stood in the road ahead of him, bathed in this dull yellowish light of the clouded moon. He stopped on the bridge and looked at her.

"What do you want?" he asked her.

"I am waiting for Harry," she said.

Harry said he begged her to tell him her name and where she lived, but she would never answer either question.

"I'm Harry," he then told her.

"Then I'll turn around and go back."

"Let me go with you," he said to her. "I'm Harry, and if you are looking for me I'll go with you."

"No," she said. "No, I must go back alone."

Harry said he ran after her and nearly killed himself trying to catch her. She was always the same distance ahead of him, no matter how hard he ran to catch her. After they had gone three miles, he suddenly woke up and jumped out of bed. After that, no matter how much he wanted to go back to sleep and recapture the dream, he was always wide awake until morning. Each time this happened he had to get up in the middle of the night, dress, and walk around the camp until daylight. He was never sleepy after the dream, although he usually slept each morning until eight-thirty or nine.

I saw Harry again the next day, but we did not speak about his dream for almost a month. Then one morning he told me he had had the dream for July. He told me about it again. It was the same as it had always been.

Then he told me something else. He said that recently, since he had been at camp that summer, he had been having the dream while he was awake. The daytime dream, as he called it, did not come at regular intervals like the one in sleep, but it was the same dream nevertheless. He would be driving his car along the country road to the village, wide awake and singing or whistling, when suddenly he saw this young girl standing in the road. When he was almost upon her, she turned and ran down the road in the direction he was going. He was never able to catch her then either, although once he speeded his car up to eighty miles an hour. She disappeared from sight three miles from the place where he first saw her. Several times he stopped the car, got out, and ran into the woods calling her.

THE DREAM

He knew that was foolish, but he said the intense attraction she held for him impelled him to go after her.

"I'm going crazy if I don't stop seeing her," he said. "The only thing that will help me now will be catching her or finding her somewhere. I've passed the point where I could forget her even if the dream should suddenly stop and never come back again. The only hope I have of remaining normal for the rest of my life is that of possessing her. That doctor said it was nothing to worry about, but I've gone beyond that now. I don't worry any longer. I've got to get her. If I don't I'll be insane in another year. It's not too late yet to save myself, because last winter and spring at home I went around with a crowd of boys and girls, had dates, went to dances, and acted perfectly naturally. But as soon as the time came to have another dream I went all to pieces."

"Maybe you saw a girl like her once, and she's your love-ideal," I said jokingly, trying to make him stop thinking about it so seriously. "You ought to try to find her when you go home this fall."

But he would never laugh about the dream. He was always serious about it, as if it were something sacred.

"There's no other girl like her. There couldn't be. No other girl could have such a voice. The sound of it is perfect, and there is a distinct meaning in the music-like notes."

"Just the same," I said, "if I were you I'd try to find one like her when you go home. You would be all right then. It would be all over. The dream would probably never come back again."

Harry walked away without answering me. The expression on his face told me that he believed I could never understand.

Near the end of August, a few days after the time for him to have the monthly dream, I went over to Harry's camp early one morning. He was sitting very still in a deep canvas campchair under the pine trees.

When he saw me he jumped up and ran to meet me.

"I had that dream again the other night," he said excitedly. His hands were shaking even more than they did the day he was painting the canoe at the boathouse. "The same dream came back again the other night."

"That's too bad," I said. "The thing for you to do now is to try every psychiatrist in the country until you are cured. Surely there is one somewhere who can help you."

"No," he said, "I don't want it to stop now. I want it to keep on coming back, because it will turn into reality. I'm going to find that girl. Last night while I was having the dream I saw a signboard nailed to a tree beside the bridge. It was there for the first time. Somebody recently put it up. It was a new sign, freshly painted and lettered. There was a big arrow on it, such as highway signs have, and over that was lettered, LOST LAKE—20 MILES."

"What does that mean?"

"That means that I will find the girl living at Lost Lake, of course. That is where she lives."

"How do you know she lives there?" I was undecided whether he was joking at last about the dream, or if he was really serious and believed that.

"Because the sign said that lake is twenty miles from the bridge. And Lost Lake is twenty miles from Rangeley, isn't it? Well, that means that the bridge is near Rangeley too. I'm going up there to find her. I might not find her the first day, but I will before I come back. She's living in a camp somewhere on Lost Lake. I know that. I'm too certain about it to be wrong."

I could not understand how he could believe that girl was up there, at least one that would be enough like her to make him believe she was the same.

"There is probably more than one lake with that name," I said. "The one you are looking for may be on the other side of the continent."

He ignored me entirely.

THE DREAM

"I'm not certain where that bridge is, but it is of no importance, because I can start from Rangeley, or from any other direction and get to the lake. You see how that could be, don't you? The important thing is to get to the lake. Then I'll start walking around it and ask at each camp for the girl. It may take me a week to go around the lake, because there is no road along the shore, but I won't be surprised if I find her at the first camp I stop at."

I was almost as excited as Harry, in spite of myself. His explanations of the sign on the tree and his interpretations of the dream would have convinced me that the girl was actually alive if my better sense had not told me it was impossible. However, I wanted to go with him, for the adventure.

"When are you starting, Harry?" I asked him. "I want to go along."

"I'm starting in the morning," he said, "but I can't take you along. I'm sorry. But you see, as soon as I find her I'm going to marry her. That's what I've been waiting for all these seven years."

"Good Lord, Harry," I said, "you don't mean to say that you believe you are going to find a girl actually enough like the one in the dream to make you think she is the same one, do you?"

He took two rings from his pocket and held them in the palm of his hand for me to see. One was a diamond solitaire, the other a wedding ring.

"I've had these for more than two years," he said. "I didn't have the nerve to show them to you before, because I knew you would laugh at me. But since I've found her I don't mind showing them to you."

"But you haven't found her yet, Harry. She may not be at Lost Lake, after all."

Harry did not say anything for several minutes. He looked at me as if he were wondering how anyone could doubt that such a girl, as he had dreamed of, was not alive that moment.

"If you don't believe what I've told you," he said, "then why don't you bet me that I won't find her?"

Whatever doubt was then left in my mind was slowly leaving me. Even at that moment I thought I saw her standing up there in the woods, at a camp on the lake, waiting for Harry to come.

"Do you want to do that?" he insisted.

"No," I said, "I'd rather not."

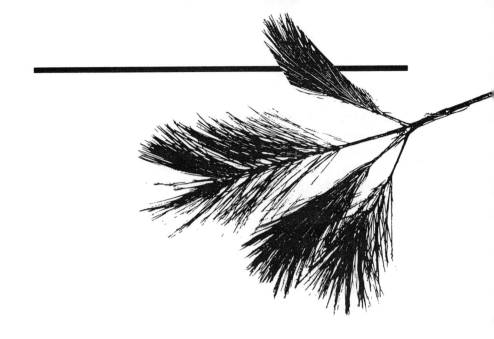

THE MIDWINTER
GUEST

It was the first time in his whole life that Orland Trask had done such a thing. Even Orland's wife could not say afterward what had got into Orland to cause him to tell the strange man from the eastern country that he might remain in the house and stay for the night. And it was the last time. Both Orland and Emma knew better than to do a thing like that again.

The stranger from the eastern country knocked on the door that evening while Orland and his wife were eating supper. Orland heard him knock at the beginning, but he did not make an effort to get up from the table to answer a knocking on his door at suppertime.

"It's nobody I want dealings with," Orland said to his wife. "A man who would come knocking on a neighbor's door at mealtime hadn't ought to be listened to. Finns and Swedes are the only people I ever heard of who didn't have better sense."

"Maybe some of the Morrises are sick, Orland," Emma said. "I'll go see."

"Stay sat in your seat, woman. Even those Morrises have got better sense than to take to illness at mealtime."

The knocking became louder. The man out there was pounding on the storm door with a heavy oak walking stick.

Orland's wife turned and looked out the window behind her. It was still snowing. The wind had died down with nightfall and the flakes were floating lightly against the panes.

The stranger at the door was impatient. He opened the storm door and banged on the panels of the house door and against the clapboards with the knotted end of his walking stick, and then he turned and beat against the door with the heels of his studded boots. He was making a lot of noise out there for a stranger, more noise than Orland had ever heard at his door.

"I'll go see," Emma said again, rising from her chair at the other end of the table.

"You stay sat in your seat, woman," Orland told her.

Orland's wife sank back into the chair, but barely had she settled herself when suddenly the door burst open with a gust of snow and icy wind, and the strange man stood there glaring at them. He was wearing black leather breeches and a red and green mackinaw and a brown fur cap pulled so far down over his ears that only his eyes and nose were showing. Snow had clung to his eyelashes and had frozen in long thin icicles that reached almost to his mouth. He stomped and blew, knocking the snow from his boots and shaking it from his cap and mackinaw. The heavy oak walking stick rapped as loudly as ever against the door sill. The man had not entered the house, but the door was open and the frosty air blew inside.

Orland's back was turned to the door and the first that he knew of the man bursting in was when the icy blast of snow and wind struck him. His wife, Emma, had seen everything from the beginning, but she was afraid to say or to do anything until Orland turned around. She knew that a man who would burst open a door would not wait to be asked into the room.

"Holy Mother," the stranger who stood in the doorway muttered, "the bones of my body are stiff as ice."

He came into the room then, his mittens under his arm, and his hands full of snow that he had scooped from the doorstep. He shut the door with the heel of his boot and walked around the table at which Orland was sitting, and rubbed his hands with the new snow.

Orland had not said a word. He sat glaring at the heavily clothed man who had entered his house unbidden.

Emma asked the strange man, guardedly, if his hands were frozen. While she waited for him to answer, she glanced again at Orland.

"Holy Mother," the stranger said again, "the bones of my body are stiff as ice."

He continued to rub the new snow over the backs of his hands and around his fingers. He still did not go near the heater in the corner.

"My name is Phelps," he said, "and I come from the eastern country of Maine. Down there the townsmen take in cold men from the frost at night."

"Well," Orland said, pushing back his chair from the table, "the townsmen in this part of the state have got the sense to stay indoors when they have no good business out in a frosty night."

Emma went to the door and brought back a bowl of new snow. She placed the bowl on the carpet in front of the stranger who had said his name was Phelps. He began to unlace his boots while Emma got ready to take away the supper dishes.

"Freeze your toes, too?" Orland said. "Any man who would walk out and freeze his hands and feet ought to have them drop off with frostbite."

Phelps removed his boots and socks and began rubbing his toes with the new snow.

"Am a poor man," Phelps said, "and I'm not a house owner. My brother wrote me a letter to come over to New Hampshire and help him peel pulpwood. Started out walking, and I've got the high mountains yet to cross. Guess you will take me in and put me up for the night."

Orland filled his pipe and struck a match before he answered. He then waited until Emma had gone into the kitchen again.

"The country would be a heap better off without fools like you walking through the snow and frost to New Hampshire in dead of winter, and it's my duty to turn you out and let the frost finish its job of freezing you. That's what I ought to do to a man who would come into a neighbor's house without asking. The country has got too many like you in it now. But my wife would take on if I was to turn you out, so I'll have to let you stay for the night. Will give you warning, though; the next time your brother writes you to come over to New Hampshire to help him peel pulpwood, it had better be before winter sets in. You won't get aid here again. Won't stand to have strangers coming into my house unbidden."

Phelps took his feet out of the new snow and put them on the sheet of newspaper Orland's wife had spread for him. He made no effort to move or to thank Orland for permitting him to stay for the night. He just sat and stared at the snow falling against the window. He was an old man, much older than Orland. He looked to be at least eighty years old. His hair was almost white, but his body was firm and muscular. If he had been less than six feet tall, he would have appeared to be overweight.

Presently Emma came back into the room and carried out the bowl of melting snow and the damp newspaper, and then she handed the old man a clean bath towel. He dried his hands and feet and put his socks and boots on again.

"Show me the place to sleep, and good night," he said wearily.

"Guess you will want the use of the spare chamber," Orland said, scowling at the old man. "Well, you're going to get it. Could give you some blankets and put you on the carpet, but I'm not. Am giving you the use of the spare chamber. My wife will fix you a plate of breakfast in the morning, if you are in here on time. Nobody eats a breakfast in my house after six-thirty."

Emma lit a lamp and showed the old man to the spare chamber. When she returned, Orland had begun reading the paper and he had nothing to say to her.

Just before he got up to go to bed, Orland called his wife.

"Give that man who said his name was Phelps a helping of beans and potatoes for breakfast," he said, "but don't give him but one plateful. Don't want to be the cause of prolonging the lives of people who walk through the snow and frost to New Hampshire in dead of winter."

Orland went to bed then, leaving Emma to clean the room and to set the chairs against the wall. He was asleep long before she had finished her work.

When Orland got up and lit the lamp the next morning at five-thirty, he listened for several minutes before calling Emma. He went to the wall that separated their room from the spare chamber and listened for a sound of the old man. The only sound that he could hear anywhere in the house was the breathing of Emma.

After calling his wife, Orland went to the kitchen range and opened the drafts and shook down the ashes. The firebox was ablaze in a minute or two, and he went to the next room and replenished the fire in the heater. Outside, it had stopped snowing during the night, and there were deep drifts of new snow.

Breakfast was ready at six-thirty, and Emma set the dishes aside on the range to wait until the old man came into the next room. She knew that Orland would call for his breakfast at almost any minute, but she delayed placing it on the table as long as she could.

"It's time for breakfast, Emma," Orland said. "Why haven't you got it ready?"

"Am putting it on the table right away," she said. "Maybe you had best go call Mr. Phelps while I'm doing it."

"Will be damned if I go call him," Orland said. "Told the old fool last evening what time breakfast was ready, and if he doesn't get up when it's ready, then I'm not going to wear out my shoes running to call him. Sit down and let's eat, Emma."

Emma sat down without a word.

After they had finished, Orland filled his pipe. He took a match from his coat pocket, but he waited a minute or longer before striking it.

"Clear away the dishes, Emma," he said.

Orland's wife carried out the dishes and plates to the kitchen. She placed the dish of beans on the range to keep them warm a while longer.

When she came back into the room for the rest of the table-ware, Orland motioned to her to listen to him. "That old fool from the eastern country and going to New Hampshire to help his brother peel pulpwood had better be setting out toward the high mountains. He's already missed the breakfast we had for him. Will give him another ten minutes, and if he's not out of the house by then, I'll throw him out, leather breeches and all."

Emma went back into the kitchen to wash the dishes while Orland filled the heater with maple chunks. One look at Orland's face was enough to frighten her out of the room.

Orland waited longer than ten minutes, and each second that passed made him more angry. It was almost eight o'clock then, an hour after breakfast was over. Orland got up and opened the house door and the storm door. His face was aflame and his motions were quick and jerky.

"Take care, woman," he said to Emma. "Take care!"

Emma came to the kitchen door and stood waiting to see what Orland was going to do. She did not know what on earth to do when Orland became as angry as he was then.

"Stand back, Emma," he said. "Stand back out of my way."

He began running around the room, looking as if he himself did not know what he was likely to do that minute or the next.

"Orland—" Emma said, standing in the kitchen door where she could get out of his way if he should turn toward her.

"Take care, woman," he shouted at her. "Take care!"

Orland was piling all the furniture in the corner of the room beside the heater. He jerked up the carpet and the rugs, pulled down the curtains, and carried all the old newspapers and magazines to the fire. He was acting strangely, Emma knew, but she did not know what on earth he was going to do nor how to stop him. She had never seen Orland act like that before in all her life, and she had lived with him for almost fifty years.

"Orland—" she said again, glancing backward to the outside kitchen door to make certain of escape.

"Take care, woman," Orland said. "Take care!"

The furniture, rugs and carpet, and newspapers were blazing like a May grass fire within a few minutes. Smoke and flame rose to the ceiling and flowed down the walls. Just when Emma thought surely that Orland would be burned alive in the fire, he ran out of the door and into the yard. She ran screaming through the other door.

Emma's first thought when she saw the house burning, was where would they live now. Then she remembered their other house, the ten-room brick house down the road near the village. Orland would not live in it because he had said that the frame house would have to be worn out before they could go to live in their brick house. He had been saying that for twenty years, and during all of that time the fine brick house of ten rooms had been standing at waste. Now, at last, they could live in it.

There were no people passing along the road so early in the morning, but John White saw the smoke and flame from his house across the flats, and he came running over with a bucket of water. By the time he got there, all the water had splashed out of the bucket, and he set it down and looked at the fire.

"Am sorry to see that, Orland," he said.

"Save your pity for some who are in need of it," Orland said.

"Well, you've got good insurance on it, anyway," John said. "That will help a lot. When you collect the insurance money, you can go and live in your brick house in style and good comfort."

"Not going to collect the insurance," Orland said.

"You're not! Why won't you collect it?"

"Because I set fire to the house myself."

"Set fire to it yourself! Good God, Orland, you must have lost your mind and reason!"

"Had a blamed good reason for doing it."

John White walked away and turned around and came back where Orland was standing. He looked at Orland and then at the burning house and at Orland again.

Orland began telling John about the old man who had said his name was Phelps. He started at the beginning, when Phelps knocked on the storm door at mealtime. Then he told John about giving the old man permission to spend the night in the house after he had walked in unbidden.

"But I told him to get up in time for breakfast at six-thirty," Orland said. "I told him that, and the old fool heard me, too. When this morning came, I waited five, ten minutes for him to come and eat. He didn't even get up out of bed. He just stayed there, sleeping. Then I sat and waited a whole hour for him to get up, but he still just stayed in the spare chamber and slept. Am not the kind to allow the country to get cluttered up with men with no more sense than to start out walking to New Hampshire in dead of winter to peel pulpwood. That old fool said he started out from somewhere in the eastern country to walk over there through the snow and frost, and he hadn't even got as far as the high mountains. If I hadn't stopped him here, he'd have gone to some town and couldn't go further. Then he'd have been a burden on the state, because there's not a town down-Maine that would have claimed him, not even a town in the eastern country would have given him citizenship."

Suddenly, Emma screamed and fell down on her back. Orland ran to see what the matter with her was.

While he was away attending to Emma, John White saw something move behind one of the windows in the spare chamber. Before he could go closer to see what it was, the roof over that part of the building fell in, sending up a shower of sparks and fragments of black embers.

Orland came back beside John and stood watching the house as it sank lower and lower to the ground.

"Lived in this town a long time," John said, "almost any man's lifetime, I guess, but I never before saw a man burn his house down just for durn meanness. Don't guess you'd have done it, if it wasn't for the fact that you own a brick house that's a lot better shelter than this frame one was."

"That old fool said he was on his way to New Hampshire to help his brother peel—"

"Well, all I've got to say is that it looks to me like you could have asked him just once to get up out of bed and clear out of the house. Doesn't appear to me like a man ought to set fire to and burn down a good frame house just because a guest won't get out of bed in time for breakfast."

"Maybe I wouldn't have done it," Orland said, "but after I had thought all night about it, there wasn't any other way to treat him. Why, that old fool who said his name was Phelps opened my door and come in without my bidding, right when I was sitting at the table at mealtime. You don't guess I'd have gone and asked him to get out of bed, do you, after he had done a thing like that?"

"Guess you would have gone and told him to get up, all right, if you hadn't been trying for nearly twenty years to find a way to move into your brick house. This frame house was just about worn out, anyway. Orland. Wasn't no sense in burning him up just to get the house down and out of your way."

"Couldn't take the risk," Orland said. "This house has always been cussed mean. It was just hardheaded enough to have stood in good repair right up to the day I took ill and died."

THE MATING OF
MARJORIE

He was coming—he was coming—God bless
him! He was coming to marry her—coming all
the way from Minnesota!

Trembling, breathless, Marjorie read the letter
again and again, holding it desperately in the ten
fingers of her hands. Then at last, her eyes so
blurred she could no longer see the handwriting,
she placed the letter against the bareness of her
breasts where she could breathe into it all the
happiness of her heart. All the way from Minnesota he was coming—coming all that great distance to marry her!

The letter's every word, every mark of careless punctuation, was burned inerasably on her memory. The thought of the letter was like a poem running through her—like the chill of sudden warmth—fragments of lines repeating themselves like the roar in a furnace-pipe.

His letter was not a proposal of marriage, but he did say he liked the way she looked in the picture she sent him. And why would he be coming all the way from Minnesota if he did not intend asking her to be his wife? Surely he wanted her.

Marjorie had his picture, too. She could actually feel the untiring strength of the lean muscles stretching over his face to the chin. Her fingers stole over his face excitedly, filling her with passion for the man with whom she would mate. He was a strong man. He would do with her as he pleased.

Surely he would like her. He was a mature man, and men who are mature seek beauty of soul and body when they marry. Marjorie was beautiful. Her beauty was her youth and charm. He wrote Marjorie that her eyes and her face and her hair were the loveliest he had ever seen. And her body was beautiful, too. He would see that when he came. Her slender limbs were cool and firm like the young pine trees in winter. Her heart was warm and eager. He would like her—surely he would.

Should she please him, and should he want her, and naturally he would when he saw her, Marjorie would give him her soul. Her soul would be her greatest gift to him. First she would give him her love, then her body, and at last her soul. No one had ever possessed her soul. But neither had her body or her love been possessed.

He had written frankly in all his letters. He said he wanted a wife. It was lonely, he said, living alone in Minnesota. Marjorie was lonesome, too. She had lived the long five years since her mother's death, alone. She understood. She had always been lonesome.

Marjorie was ready for love. She was twenty-four. Her arms and legs were cool and firm like the young pine trees in winter.

Her breasts and lips were warm and soft, and her breath was like the November winds that blew across the lake through the pines and firs. Marjorie was ready for love. Her lips were soft and her body was firm.

Marjorie prepared a room for him and waited his coming. She laundered the linen sheets and pillow-cases three times. They were soft like her lips and the fiber was impregnated with the odor of pines like her breath. She dried the linen each time on the limbs of the fir trees and ironed it in the early morning while it was still damp with the pine-scented air.

The day of his coming Marjorie was awake long before the sun rose. The sun rose cool and swift.

Before laying out the new clothes she would wear for him, she ran to the room and patted the pillows and smoothed the coverlet for the last time. Then hurriedly she dressed and drove to the depot nineteen miles away.

He arrived on the noon train from Boston. He was much larger than she had expected him to be, and he was much more handsome than she had hoped.

"Are you Marjorie?" he asked huskily.

"Yes," Marjorie answered eagerly. "I am Marjorie. You are Nels?"

"Yes," he smiled, his eyes meeting hers. "I am Nels."

Marjorie led Nels to the automobile. They got in and drove away. Nels was a silent man, speaking crisply and infrequently. He looked at Marjorie all the time. He looked at her hands and face intently. She was nervous and self-conscious under his non-committal scrutiny. After they had gone several miles he placed his arm across the back of the seat. Only once or twice did Marjorie feel his arm. The bumpy roads tossed them both as the car sped across-country. Nels' arms were as strong and muscular as a woodsman's.

Late that afternoon Marjorie and Nels walked down through the wood to the lake. There was a cold icy wind out of the northeast and the lake rose and tossed as if a storm were upon it. While they stood on a boulder at the lakeside watching the waves, a sudden gust of wind threw her against his shoulder. Nels braced her with his steel-like arms and jumped to the ground. Later she showed Nels the icehouse and pointed out to him the shed where the boats were stored in winter. Then they walked home through the pines and firs.

While Marjorie prepared supper Nels sat in the parlor smoking his pipe. Several times Marjorie ran to the open door for a hurried glimpse of the man she was to marry. The only motion about him was the steady flow of tobacco-smoke boiling from the bowl of his pipe. When the meal was ready Marjorie quickly changed her dress and called Nels. Nels enjoyed the meal before him. He liked the way she had prepared the fish. Her skin was so hot she could not bear to press her knees together. Nels ate with full appetite.

After Marjorie had hastily carried the dishes to the kitchen she again changed her dress and went into the room where Nels sat by the fireplace. They sat in silence until she brought him the album and showed him the pictures. He looked at them silently.

All through the evening she sat hoping he would soon take her in his arms and kiss her. He would later, of course, but she wanted now to be in his arms. He did not look at her.

At ten-thirty Nels said he should like to go to bed. Marjorie jumped up and ran to his room. She turned back the pine-scented covers and smoothed the pillows. Bending over the bed, she laid her flushed cheek against the cool soft linen. Suppose she should hide in the bed and Nels found her there—what would happen! Tearing herself away, she went back into the room where Nels sat silently by the fire.

After Nels had gone to his room and closed the door behind him Marjorie went to her own bedroom. She sat down in a rocking-chair and looked out upon the lake. It was after midnight when she got up and undressed. Just before retiring she tiptoed to the door of Nels' room. She stood there several minutes listening intensely. Her fingers touched the door softly. He did not hear her. He was asleep.

Marjorie was awake at five. Nels came into the kitchen at seven while she prepared breakfast. He was freshly clean, and under his loose tweed suit she all but felt the great strength of his body.

"Good-morning," he said.

"Good-morning, Nels," she greeted him eagerly.

After breakfast they sat in the parlor while Nels smoked his pipe. When he finished smoking he stood up before the fire-place. He took out his watch and glanced at the time. Marjorie sat hushed behind him.

"What time does the train leave for Boston?" he asked.

With stilled breath she told him.

"Will you take me to the train?" he asked her.

She said she would.

Marjorie immediately went into the kitchen and leaned heavily against the table. Nels remained in the parlor re-filling his pipe. Marjorie ran toward the parlor several times, but each time she turned back when she reached the door. She wanted to ask Nels if he were coming back. She picked up a plate and it crashed to the floor. It was the first piece of china she had broken since the morning of her mother's death. Trembling, she put on her hat and coat. Of course he was coming back! How foolish it was to think he would not! He was probably going to Boston to get some presents for her. He would come back—of course he would!

When they reached the depot Nels held out his hand. She placed her hand in his. It was the first time his skin had touched her skin.

"Good-bye," he said.

"Good-bye, Nels," she smiled at him. "I hope you enjoyed your visit."

Nels picked up his travelling-bag and started towards the waiting-room.

Marjorie's arms and legs had the numbness of death in them. She started the motor uncertainly. He had not said he would return!

"Nels!" she cried desperately, gripping the door of the automobile with bloodless fingers.

Nels stopped and turned around, facing her.

"Nels, you are welcome to come back any time you want to," she begged unashamedly.

"Thank you," he replied briefly, "but I'm going home to Minnesota and I'll not be back again."

"What!" she cried, her lips quivering so violently she could barely make them speak. "Where are you going——?"

"To Minnesota," he replied in a phrase.

Marjorie drove home as fast as her car would take her. As soon as she reached the house she ran to Nels' room.

In Nels' room Marjorie stood by the side of the bed and looked at the crumpled sheets and pillows with tear-blinded eyes. With a sob she tore off her clothes and threw herself between the sheets where Nels had lain. In her arms she hugged the pillows and dampened them with her tears. She could feel his body against hers. She kissed his face and held her lips for him to kiss.

It was night when she arose from the bed. The sun had gone down and the day was over. Only the cool clear twilight was left to shadow the room.

Throwing a blanket around her shoulders, Marjorie jerked the sheets and pillow-cases from the bed and ran blindly to her own room. She opened the cedar chest and tenderly folded the crumpled sheets and pillow-cases. She laid the linen in the chest and dragged the chest to the side of her bed.

Marjorie turned out the light and lay down between the sheets of her own bed.

"Good-night, Nels," she whispered softly, her fingers touching the smooth lid of the cedar chest at her side.

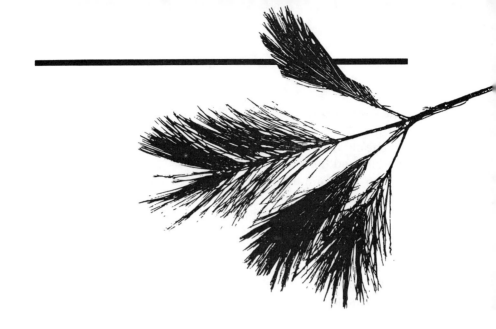

THE LONELY DAY

For a week the wet midsummer mists had been creeping over Maine from the south, from the coast; sheets of low-hanging gray vapor spread over the country like dirty steam and levelled the foothills into smooth fields, while the mountains had been wrapped in wet gray clouds and put away from sight towards the north, towards Canada. Yesterday the mists had lifted over the housetop, almost over the tops of the elm trees; but to-day, Sunday, the lower air was so wet that the meshes of the window-screens were filled with panes of opaque water.

Katherine hurried across the wet grass from the garden and went into the house. She opened the kitchen-door quietly and closed it slowly as she stood back against it.

The old woman struck at her with the heavy end of the crutch and cursed her.

The girl jumped away and ran to the other side of the kitchen.

The room was wet with the midsummer mists. There were little balls of water in the dusty spider-web over the stove and a thin stream of water trickled at intervals down the table-legs to the floor.

"Go pick me some berries," the old woman cried at her. "GO PICK ME SOME BERRIES!" she shouted. "Do you hear me? You damned little sneak! Bring me a pail of berries before I take this crutch and kill you!"

"All right," Katherine whimpered. "I'm going."

"Well, why don't you run? I'll break your head if you don't get out of here after those berries!"

Katherine took the berry-pail from the kitchen-table and ran outside before the old woman could strike her again. The wet mists clung to her hair as she ran towards the pasture, and tears fell on her dampened cheeks. The berry-field was on the other side of the stream, beyond the sheep pasture. Bordering the field was the State road, running north and south.

She gathered the wet berries as quickly as she could. She knew the old woman was even then waiting at the kitchen-door to strike her with the crutch because she had not re-turned sooner. She tried as hard as she could, but she could not pick them any faster.

Several hundred yards away automobiles passed in both directions, going up into the Provinces, coming back into Maine. All around her was the forest, the deep dark forest where men worked in winter, in the white frozen snow, cut-ting pulpwood. The men who worked there were French from Canada and she could not understand what they said. Now there was nobody near. The closest settlement was forty miles to the south and the only people who came through the woods were tourists, passing but never stopping. She had never gone so far as the road, but when she picked berries she could hear the roar of the speeding automobiles and occasionally the laughter of men and women. The old woman would not let her go near the road.

While she was gathering the wet berries she thought she heard one of the automobiles stop. As she listened, there came shouts and laughter from the direction of the road, but she was too far away to hear what the people said. She bent over the berry-bushes and tried to fill the pail as quickly as she could.

It was noon before the pail was full. She ran towards the house where the old woman sat waiting for the berries.

While she ran down the hillside towards the stream in the sheep pasture she heard again the shouts and laughter of several persons. When she reached the footbridge she could see them in dim outline through the mists. There were five or six men and girls farther down the stream toward the lower lake.

Katherine crossed the footbridge and went down the stream where the men and girls were. At first she thought they were fishing, but almost before she knew it, she was within a hundred yards of them; and then she saw that they were swimming and diving into the stream. The low-hanging cloud had cleared along the banks of the stream for a few moments and she saw them plainly only a short distance away.

She stared wild-eyed as she saw one of the men and a girl wade out of the water and stand on the bank a moment before diving in again. Then others came out to dive and she saw that none of them was wearing a bathing-suit.

She was so confused by what she saw that she could neither cry out nor run away. Her heart was beating madly and her body trembled with excitement.

While she stood in amazement before the scene, one of the girls climbed to the bank of the stream and ran out across the pasture. The girl turned and called to one of the men.

"You can't catch me, Jimmy!"

Laughing, the naked girl ran off and disappeared in the heavy mists.

"I'll catch you if I don't catch a cow first!" the man shouted after her.

The other men and girls were laughing and splashing water in the stream.

Suddenly the girl who had disappeared in the misty pasture cried out:

"Oh, Jimmy, come quick and find me! I've caught a sheep!"

"I can't, Helen!" the man called to her. "I'm all tangled up in a wire fence!"

The other men and girls climbed to the bank of the stream, shouting ridiculous suggestions telling how to hold a sheep and how to get out of a wire fence. They all fell down on the grass hysterical with laughter.

Katherine stood beside the stream, above them. She had never seen anything such as this happen before in her life, and she could barely believe that men and girls could have such a good time together. It was too incredible to be true, but she could hear everything they said and see everything they did. And still the scene was unreal to her. She had never been with men and girls of her own age, and she was bewildered with the strangeness of their behavior.

Her heart was racing so excitedly that she could stand still no longer. She wanted to run as fast as she could and fall in the midst of those men and girls and laugh with them. Then suddenly she felt the weight of the berry-pail in her hand, and she turned and ran as quickly as she could to the house where the old woman waited.

The old woman snatched the pail of berries from her hands and began eating the fruit. Katherine went to her room and closed the door. She stood beside her bed trembling with excitement, remembering what she had seen and heard down at the stream in the sheep pasture. She ran from window to window trying to see through the wet mists. If only there had been no mists, she knew she could have seen the men and girls in the pasture. But she could see no further than the windows. The mists covered everything outside.

While the old woman sat in the kitchen eating the berries, Katherine slipped quietly from the front of the house and ran towards the stream. As she ran down the hillside she tried to hear the things the men and girls were saying. She wanted to run, just as they were, into their midst and throw herself on the grass beside them. She wanted to laugh and dive into the stream and splash water over everybody.

Running wildly towards the stream, she suddenly saw that the men and girls were not there. They had taken their clothes and gone back to the automobile to dress, and by now they were probably several miles away. Now there was nothing she could do. She did not want to stay at the stream alone. She wanted to be with someone, with men and girls who laughed and splashed water, and to have them see her. Alone, she stood crying by the stream. Once she looked at herself, but she was alone. She wanted men to see her, and girls, and she wanted to see them.

The wet mists chilled her body and she began to shiver. The warm tears fell cold and hard on her arms and hands.

Slowly she turned and walked up the hillside towards the house. She repeated over and over the words she thought she had heard as she was running so happily to the stream a few minutes before.

The old woman had not missed her. She still sat in the kitchen eating from the pail the berries Katherine had picked that morning.

Katherine sat on the bed in her room crying. She fell backward and crushed a pillow over her face so the old woman could not hear her.

Later in the afternoon she got up and undressed. She walked around the room, stopping at a window and trying to penetrate the gray mists that hung over the earth. But taking off her clothes, putting them on, taking them off again was not enough.

There was no one to see her, there were no men and girls she could see. It was not what had happened in the sheep pasture that morning, when the gray mists were filled with laughter and the stream with splashing water. It was not the same thing. And she could not laugh aloud.

After supper, when the old woman had gone to bed, Katherine stole out of the house and ran through the wet dark night towards the pasture. When she reached the stream, she could see nothing, not even the grass at her feet. All about her she felt the clinging wet clouds of vapor. The black mists covered everything. Over the hill she thought she heard an automobile speed along the road towards the Provinces. Her nightgown had fallen at her feet on the wet grass, but she could not keep from feeling that she had not taken off as much as the men and girls had that afternoon. She pulled at her arms and waist as if she expected to find something else to throw off from her. She tried again, but she could not laugh aloud in the wet mists.

She ran across the berry-field until she reached the road where the automobiles passed. When she got there she stood in the road and waited. It was then after midnight. She waited but no car came from either direction.

While she stood in the center of the road she distinctly heard in the distance the same laughter that had made her so excited that afternoon. Clearly she heard a girl's voice. Someone was calling, "You can't catch me, Jimmy!" Almost immediately the voice of a man could be heard out in the far darkness somewhere, "I'll catch you if I don't catch a cow first!" And then, all around her, men and girls were shouting and laughing, just as she had heard them that afternoon in the pasture. From the music of their voices she knew they were splashing water in a stream and lying naked on the grassy banks beside the water. But they were so far away she knew she could never find them while everything was so black and misty.

She waited and listened for an automobile to come up or down the road. But there was none. It was after midnight. She wanted to stand in the center of the road and have the men and women see her.

The first light of day broke through the mists and found her lying in the road, her body made lifeless by an automobile that had shot through the darkness an hour before. She was without motion, but she was naked, and a smile that was the beginning of laughter made her the most beautiful woman whom tourists speeding to the Provinces had ever seen.

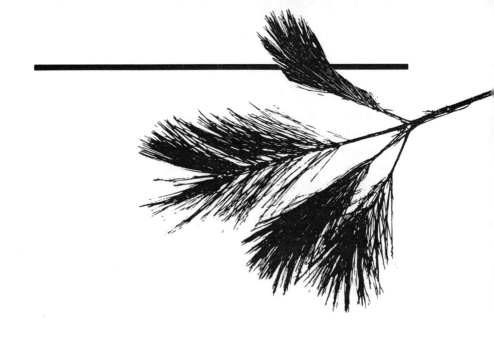

JOHN THE INDIAN
AND GEORGE HOPKINS

George Hopkins, who was about ninety years old, died just in time to have his grave decorated on Memorial Day. Grace and Jessie, his two daughters, buried him on the hilltop behind the house and had an iron fence put around the plot. Grace Hopkins, who was several years the older, said she wanted the fence painted red. Jessie, the younger one, said it was going to be left just as it was. They argued about the fence for two days, and then Grace lost her temper and called Jessie ugly names and had the iron fence painted red anyway. Jessie took her half of the furniture from the house and moved to another part of town.

Grace stayed where she was and had another coat of red paint put on the fence around George Hopkins' grave.

Nobody in the town paid much attention to what the Hopkins girls were doing, because the whole Hopkins family had been raising the devil for the past twenty years or more.

George Hopkins had been a selectman ever since anybody could remember and he had always scrapped with some one over something.

First it was over the question whether the town should buy a snowplow and keep the main roads open in winter. He had said "No!" the first time, and had kept on saying that at every town meeting.

"Let the snow be!" he shouted. "God melts it every spring and don't make no charge for it!"

Another time he was scrapping with one of the boys from the village who wanted to come and sit up evenings with one of his daughters.

"You get the hell away from here, Tom Peck's son," he told the boy, "and don't you come back unless you've got a marriage license in your pocket."

George Hopkins had been a mean old scoundrel.

Friday before Memorial Day, Jessie brought her lawn-mower and handscythe and went up the hill to where they had buried her father. She cut the grass with the mower and trimmed the edges of the plot where the grass grew against the fence. When she finished she stuck a flag in the center of the mound and tied a wreath around the headstone.

Grace heard about Jessie going to the grave, so she got her lawn-mower and grass-clippers and went up the hill. The plot was in fine shape, but Grace went to work and mowed the grass over again and clipped around the edges where it grew between the iron palings of the fence. She jerked the wreath from the headstone and put one of her own making in its place. She pulled up Jessie's flag and stuck a larger one near the headstone and a smaller one near the footstone.

John the Indian and George Hopkins

By nightfall Jessie had heard about Grace's going to the grave. She went over at once to John the Indian's. John lived by himself and wove baskets for sale.

She told John she wanted him to do some work for her and he agreed to help her by the hour. After supper that night he went over to Jessie's.

She brought John into the house and told him exactly what she wanted him to do. Then they went across the pasture to the hill where George Hopkins was buried. They carried a pick and shovel with them and began to open up the grave as soon as they got there. John worked for nearly two hours before he reached the coffin. George Hopkins had been buried deep so the frost would not reach him that winter.

It was hard work getting at the casket. There was no light to work by and John could not see very well after he had dug three or four feet into the ground. When he did get to the coffin, he said he would have to open it up where it was and lift George Hopkins out. It was the only thing to do. He could not get the casket out of the hole by himself.

John was a strong Indian and he got the body on top of the ground. Then he hoisted it on his shoulder and carried it to Jessie's house. Jessie came behind, bringing the pick and shovel.

Jessie told John to lay the body down by the icehouse while she looked for a place to dig the new grave. She wanted the grave near the house so she could keep watch over it from her window. She stumbled around in the dark several minutes before deciding where the new grave should be.

"Dig it here," Jessie said, standing over the place she had decided upon. "Come here, John, and dig it here."

John spat on his hands and measured off the grave with the pick-handle.

"George Hopkins a lot of damn trouble," he grunted, digging away in the dark.

John dug away in the dark. He worked for nearly an hour and then struck a ledge of rock. It was as deep as he could go without blasting. Jessie found another place for the grave and John started all over again. He dug to about the same depth in the ground and struck the same ledge. Jessie made him begin a third time, and he hit the ledge of rock again. By this time it was getting late. John was tired and Jessie said her feet were wet. She said she was afraid of catching cold and pneumonia. John said he was going home.

"What you do with that?" he asked, pointing toward the icehouse. George Hopkins sat propped up against it.

Jessie said she did not know what to do with it. She asked John what could she do with it.

"I take him home with me to-night and bring him back to-morrow night," he suggested.

"All right, John," Jessie said, much relieved. "You take it home with you and bring it back to-morrow evening after supper."

Jessie went into the house and went to bed.

John lifted the body on his shoulder and started home at a trot. The body was not too heavy for him, but it slipped around on his shoulder. It was difficult for him to keep it there. Whenever he grasped it tighter it slid away under the suit of clothes as if the skin were loose.

John got it home though. He laid it on the floor beside his bed and went to sleep.

The next morning, when he got up, he carried it to the kitchen while he cooked his breakfast.

"Want some fried potatoes for eating, George Hopkins?" John asked the body he had propped up against the woodbox.

"Huh, huh," John chuckled, "George Hopkins, you don't eat much these days."

He went about getting his breakfast.

"Maybe you want to smoke your pipe, George Hopkins," John said. "Huh, huh, George Hopkins, I got fine tobacco."

Grace went to the hilltop that forenoon to see if Jessie had been back with another wreath of her own. Grace was determined to take them away as fast as Jessie brought them.

When she reached the top of the hill and saw the pile of fresh earth inside the fenced plot, she turned around and ran straight across the town to the village as fast as she could. She went straight for a warrant.

Grace got the warrant and the man to serve it on Jessie. They went in a hurry to Jessie's house. All the doors and windows were locked tightly and they could not get in. Jessie heard them banging on the door but she would not come out. Grace and the man found the graves Jessie and John the Indian had started, but they could not find George Hopkins in any of them.

Grace came back again the next day and looked for the body but she could not find it anywhere on the place. Jessie still would not come out of the house.

John was becoming tired of waiting for Jessie to come out of the house so they could bury George Hopkins. He did not know what to do about it. He waited another two days for her to come out and by that time he was sorry he had taken the job to dig a new grave for George Hopkins. John's house was beginning to have a bad odor.

Early the next morning he went to Jessie's house and tried to make her open the door and tell him what to do. She did not make a sound. He knew she was inside because once he saw her looking at him from behind a curtain at the window.

John trotted back to his house and carried the body down to the lake and propped it up in a canoe. Then he towed it to the middle of the lake with his other canoe. He had some live bait with him and a fishing-pole.

When he reached the center of the lake he threw the baited fishing-line overboard, tied the pole securely to the canoe George Hopkins was in, and shoved away from it.

John paddled to the shore, leaving George Hopkins sitting up in the canoe salmon-fishing. He looked back just as he reached the shore and saw the canoe shoot down the lake fast as a speedboat. A big bull-headed salmon had hooked the line. The salmon was taking George Hopkins down the lake so fast the wind blew his hat overboard.

John the Indian waited on the shore chuckling to himself until they were out of sight. Then he went home to get himself some breakfast.

THE GRASS FIRE

During the last week of April nobody with any
sense at all would have gone out and deliberately
set fire to a hayfield. There had been no rainfall
since the March thaw and the country was as
dry as road dust in midsummer. The farmers
who had fields that needed burning over were
waiting for a heavy shower of rain to come and
soak the ground thoroughly before they dared
begin the spring firing.

Carl Abbott had been in the habit of burning
over his fields the last week of April for the past
thirty years and he said that he was not going to
start that late in his life letting his new crop hay

be ruined by raspberry bushes and gray-birch seedlings if he knew anything about it. The people in the town thought he was merely talking to himself again to make himself heard, and that he really had the good sense to keep fire away from dry grass until a hard rain had come. Carl was always talking about the way he stuck to his lifelong habits, and people never paid much attention to him any more, anyway.

It was late in the afternoon when Carl got ready to fire the field on the north side of his farm. He carried two buckets of water with him, and a broom, and went up the side road to the north field.

When he reached the gate, he saw Jake Thompson come driving down the backroad. Carl tried to get through the gate and behind the stone wall before Jake saw him, but he could not hide himself quickly enough because of the two buckets of water he was carrying, and his wooden leg.

"Hey there!" Jake called, whipping up his horse. "What you doing in that hayfield?"

Carl waited until Jake drove up to the gap in the wall. He put the buckets down and leaned against the broom handle.

"I'm standing here looking at you," Carl told him. "But I'm already tired of doing that, and so now I'm going in here and fire my hayfield."

"Why! you damned old fool," Jake said, "don't you know that you'll burn up your whole farm if you do that now? Feel that wind—it'll carry flame down across that meadow and into that wood lot before you know which way to look. Nobody with any sense would fire a hayfield until after a good heavy rain comes and soaks the ground."

"I didn't ask for the loan of any of your advice," Carl said.

"And I don't generally pass it around to every damn fool I meet, either," Jake said, "but I hate to have to sit here and see a man burn up all he's got and ever will have. The town's not going to raise money to waste on supporting you. There's too many just like you living on the town already."

"Guess I can live on the town if I've a mind to. Been paying taxes for thirty years and more."

"If it was left up to me," Jake said, "I'd dig a big hole in the ground and cover you up in it. And I'm man enough left to do it, too."

Carl stooped over and picked up the water buckets.

"Didn't you hear about that grass fire over in the east part of town day before yesterday?" Jake asked. "A man over there set fire to his hayfield and it got loose from him and burned up his wife."

"That's nothing to concern me," Carl said. "Haven't got a wife, and never felt the need for one. It's people with wives who do all the fool things in the world, anyway."

"Guess you're right about that," Jake said. "I was about to let it slip my mind that your daddy had a wife."

Carl turned around with the water buckets and walked a dozen yards out into the field. The dead grass was almost waist high, and it cracked and waved in the wind like chaff in a hay barn. Each time Carl took a step in the dead grass a puff of dust rose up behind him and blew away in the wind. Carl was beginning to believe that Jake was right after all. He had not realized how dry the country really was.

Jake drove his horse and buggy to the side of the road and crossed his legs. He sat back to wait and see how big a fool Carl Abbott really was.

"If you go and fire that hayfield, you'd better go take out some insurance on your stock and buildings. They won't be worth a dime otherwise; though I guess if I was hard put to it, I could give you a dollar for the ashes, including yours. They'd make the finest kind of top dressing for my potato field this year."

"If you've got any business of your own, why don't you go and attend to it?" Carl said. "Didn't invite you to stay here."

"By God, I pay just as many taxes for the upkeep of the town's roads as you do, Carl Abbott. Shall stand here until I get good and ready to go somewhere else."

Carl always said something or did something to make Jake angry whenever they got within sight or hearing distance of each other.

Jake crossed his legs again and snapped the leaves of a birch seedling with his horsewhip.

The wind was coming down from the northeast, but it shifted so frequently that nobody could have determined its true direction. In the month of April there was no way of finding out which way the wind was blowing. Jake had said that in April the wind came in all directions, except straight up, and that if man were to dig a hole in the ground it would come that way, too.

Carl stooped over in the grass and struck a match on the seat of his pants. He held the flame close to a tuft of grass and weathered it with his hands.

The flame flared up so quickly and so suddenly that it jumped up through his arms and singed his whiskers before he could get out of the way. The wind was true in the east just then, and it was blowing at about thirty miles an hour. The flame died down almost as suddenly as it had flared up, and a column of white smoke coiled straight upward for a few feet before it was caught in the wind and carried down over the meadow. The fire was smoldering in the dead grass, and the white smoke showed that it was feeding on the crisp dry tufts that grew around the stems like powder puffs. A hayfield could never be burned over completely if it were not for the small coils of grass that curled in tufts close to the ground. When the tufts blazed, the long waist-high stems caught and burned through. Then the tall grass fell over as if it were being mown with a scythe, and the fire would be under way, feeding itself far faster than any number of men could have done.

Jake Thompson watched the white smoke boil and curl in the air. He saw Carl walk over to one of the buckets and souse the broom in the water, taking all the time he wished. Then he went back to the fire and stood looking at it smolder in the tufts.

THE GRASS FIRE

A fairly new, well-sewn house broom and a pail or two of water was the finest kind of fire-fighting equipment in a hay-field. But farmers who burned over hayfields rarely undertook such a task without having three or four men to help keep the fire under control. Six men who knew how to souse a broom in a bucket of water at the proper time, keeping it sufficiently wet so the broom-straw would not catch on fire, could burn over the largest hayfield in the state. Water alone would not even begin to put out a grass fire; it was the smothering of the flame with the broad side of the broom that kept it from spreading. But nobody with any sense at all would have thought of firing a field that year until a rain had come and made the ground moist and dampened the grass tufts. Under those conditions a field would have burned so slowly that one man could have kept it under control.

Jake knew that Carl did not have a chance in the world of being able to check that fire once it had got under way.

The white smoke was boiling upward in a column the size of a barrelhead by that time. The wind had shifted again, circling around Carl's back and blowing down across the meadow from a new angle. The grass tops bowed under the force of the wind, and the wind was changing so frequently that it kept the field waving first in one and then in some other direction. Carl looked around and overhead as if by that he were doing some-thing that would cause the wind to die down into a breeze.

Jake crossed his legs again and waited to see what was going to happen next. Carl Abbott was without doubt the biggest fool he had ever known.

Suddenly the flames shot into the air higher than Carl's head and began leaping across the field towards the meadow like a pack of red foxes let loose. Carl jumped backward, stumbling, and overturning one of the buckets of water. The flames bent over under the force of the wind until they looked as if they were lying flat on top of the grass. That made the field burn even faster still, the leaping flame setting fire to the grass quicker than the eye could follow. It had been burning no longer than two or three minutes, but in that short time it had spread out into the shape of a quarter cut of pie, and it was growing larger and larger each second. Carl ran around in circles, his wooden leg sticking into the ground and tripping him with nearly every step. He would have to stop every step or two and take both hands to pull the wooden peg out of the ground.

"Hey there, Carl Abbott!" Jake shouted at him above the roar of the burning grass. "What in hell are you doing out there! Get away from that fire!"

Carl heard Jake but he paid no attention to what he said. He was trying to beat out the fire with his wet broom, but his work was not checking the flames in any direction. He was so excited that, instead of beating at the flames, most of the time he was holding the broom in the fire, and hitting the water buckets with his wooden leg. The broom caught on fire, and then he did not know which way to turn. When he did succeed in hitting at the fire with the broom, as fast as he smothered one tuft of grass it caught fire again almost immediately. In the meantime two or three fresh ones blazed up beside it.

"Come out of there, you damn fool!" Jake shouted at him. "You'll be cooked and ready to eat if you don't get out of that fire!"

Carl's hat had fallen off and had already burned into a handful of gray ashes. His whiskers were singed close to his face, making him appear at a distance as if he had had a shave, and his peg leg was charred. If he had stood still all the time he would not have been hurt, because the fire would have burned away from him; but Carl ran right into the hottest part of it, almost out of sight in the smoke and flame. His woolen pants were smoking, his coat was dropping off in smoking pieces, and a big black circle was spreading on his shirt where a spark had ignited the blue cotton cloth.

Jake jumped out of his buggy and ran into the hayfield calling Carl. He could not sit there and see a man burn himself alive, even if the man was Carl Abbott.

THE GRASS FIRE

He grabbed Carl and dragged him away from the flame and threw him down on the ground where the grass had already burned over. Carl's wooden leg was burned completely through, and as he fell to the ground it broke off in half. All that was left of it was a charred pointed stub about six or eight inches long. Carl had made the peg himself, and, instead of using oak as Jake had advised him to do, he had made it out of white pine because, he said, it would be lighter to carry around. Jake dragged him by the collar to the gap in the stone wall and dumped him in the road. Carl tried to stand up, forgetting the burned-off peg, and he tumbled over into the drain ditch and lay there helplessly.

"You would go ahead and act like a damn fool, after all, wouldn't you?" Jake said. "It's a pity I didn't let you stay out there and make ashes. They would have been worth more than you are alive. Meat ashes make the finest kind of dressing for any kind of crop."

Carl sat up and looked through the gap in the stone wall at the smoking hayfield. The fire line had already reached the wood lot, and flame was beginning to shoot from the top of the pines and hemlocks. Two hundred yards farther away were Carl's buildings. He had a team of horses in the barn, and a cow. There would be no way in the world to save them once the fire had reached the barn and caught the dry hay.

Jake tossed Carl a stick and watched him hobble the best he could down the road towards his house and buildings.

"What are we going to do?" he begged Jake. "We can't let my stock and buildings burn up, too."

"What we?" Jake said. "You and who else? You're not talking to me, because I'm having nothing to do with all this mess. I told you what not to do when you came up here a little while ago, but you were so damn smart I couldn't get anything through your head. That's why I'm having nothing at all to do with all this mess."

Carl protested feebly. He tried to get up and run down the road, but he fell each time he attempted to stand up.

"Why! do you think I'd have people saying that they passed your place and saw me helping you put out a grass fire when nobody with any sense at all would ever have started one in this kind of weather? People in this town know I don't associate with crazy men. They know me better than that. That's why I don't want them to think I've lost my mind and gone plumb crazy with you."

Carl opened his mouth, but Jake had not finished.

"I wouldn't even spit on a blade of witch grass now if I thought it would help check that fire you started. Why! the townspeople would think I had a hand in starting it, if I went and helped you check it. Nobody would believe me if I tried to tell them I begged you not to fire your field in the beginning, and then went right out and helped you fight it. The townspeople have got better sense than to believe a tale like that. They know I wouldn't do a fool thing like you went and did. They know that I have better sense than to go out and start a fire in a hayfield when it hasn't rained yet this spring. I'm no fool, Carl Abbott, even if it does appear that I'm associating with one now."

"But you can't let my stock and buildings burn up," Carl said. "You wouldn't do that, would you, Jake? I've been a fair and honest friend of yours all my life, haven't I, Jake? And didn't I cast my vote for you when you wanted to be road commissioner?"

"So I can't, can't I? Well, you just stand there and watch me try to save your stock and buildings! And this is no time to be talking politics, either. Wouldn't help you, anyway, not after the way you did there in that hayfield. I told you not to go and fire that field, and you went right ahead like a damn fool and struck a match to it, just as if I had been talking to myself away over in another part of town. No! I'm not going to do anything about it except talk. When the townspeople ask me how your farm and buildings came to catch on fire and burn up your stock and wood lot, I'll tell them you fired it."

Carl found a heavier stick and hobbled down the road towards his house and buildings. The fire had already run through the wood lot by that time, and, as they came around the bend in the road, flame was licking at the house and barn.

Jake walked behind Carl, coming down the road, and led his horse instead of riding in the buggy. He watched Carl try to run, and he thought once of putting him into the buggy, but he did not like the idea of doing that. Townspeople would say he was riding Carl around in his horse and buggy while the stock and buildings burned up.

When they got closer to the house, the roof was ablaze, and the barn was smoking. The hay in there was dry, and it looked as if it would burst into flame any second. Carl hobbled faster when he saw his buildings burning.

"Help me get my stock out, Jake," he begged. "You won't let my stock burn up, will you, Jake?"

Jake tied his horse to a tree beside the road and ran across the yard to the barn. He could not stand there and see a team of horses and a cow burn alive, even if they did belong to Carl Abbott. He ran to the barn and jerked open the stall doors.

An explosion of smoke, dust, and flame burst into his face, but the two horses and the cow bounded out the moment the stall doors were thrown open. The horses and cow ran across the yard and leaped over the brush by the roadside and disappeared into the field on the other side.

Jake knew it was a stroke of chance that enabled him to save the stock, because if the horses and cow had been farther in the barn, nothing could have induced them to leave it. The only way they could have been saved would have been to blindfold them and lead them out, and there would have been no time for that. The flame had already begun to reach the stalls.

Carl realized by that time that there was no chance of saving anything else. He saw the smoke and flame leap through the roof of the barn the moment that Jake had opened the stall doors. He felt terribly sick all over.

Jake went over to the tree and untied his horse. He climbed into the buggy and sat down. Carl stood looking at his burning buildings, and he was trying to lean on the big stick he had found up the backroad.

Jake whipped up his horse and started home. Carl turned around and saw him leave, but he had nothing to say.

"Whoa!" Jake said to his horse, pulling on the reins. He turned around in the buggy seat and called to Carl. "Well, I guess you'll have better sense than to do a thing like that again, won't you? Next time maybe you will be anxious to take some advice."

Carl glared at Jake, and turned with nothing to say to stand and watch the fire. Then suddenly he shouted at Jake.

"By God, the hayfield is burned over, ain't it?" he said, hobbling away. "Well, that's what I set out to do at the start."

Jake whipped up his horse and started for home. When he looked back for the last time, he saw Carl whittling on a pole. Carl had cut down a young pine and he was trimming it to replace the peg that had burned off in the hayfield. He wished to make the new one out of oak, but oak was the kind of wood that Jake had told him to use in the first place.

MIDSUMMER
PASSION

Middle-aged Ben Hackett and the team, Cromwell and Julia, were haying to beat hell when the
thunder-storm broke on the east ridge. Ben
knew it was coming, because all morning the
thunder had rumbled up and down the river; but
Ben did not want the storm to break until he had
drawn the hay to the barn, and when the deluge
was over he felt like killing somebody. Ben had
been sweating-hot before the storm came and
now he was mad. The rain-water cooled him
and took some of the anger out of him. But he
still swore at the thunder-storm for ruining his
first-crop hay.

The storm had passed over and the sun came out again as hot as ever, but just the same he had to throw off the load of hay he had on the rack. Swearing and sweating, Ben unloaded and drove Cromwell and Julia across the hayfield into the lane. Ben filled his pipe and climbed up on the hayrack. Clucking like a hen with a new brood of chicks, Ben urged the team toward the highroad half a mile away. The sun was out, and it was hot again. But the hay was wet. Damn it all!

"If God knows all about making hay in this kind of weather, He ought to come down and get it in Himself, by Jesus," Ben told Cromwell and Julia.

Cromwell swished his horsehairs in Ben's face and Julia snorted some thistle-down out of her nose.

Glaring up at the sky and sucking on his pipe, Ben was almost thrown to the ground between the team when Cromwell and Julia suddenly came to a standstill.

"Get along there, Cromwell!" Ben growled at the horse. "What's ailing you, Julia!"

The horse and mare moved a pace and again halted. Ben stood up, balancing himself on the hayrack.

"By Jesus!" he grunted, staring down the lane.

An automobile, unoccupied, blocked the narrow trail.

Ben climbed down, swearing to Cromwell and Julia. He paced around the automobile uncertainly, inspecting it belligerently. No person was in sight.

"Damn a man who'd stand his auto ablocking the lane," Ben grumbled, glancing at Cromwell and Julia for confirmation. "I guess I'll have to push the thing out of the way myself. By Jesus, if whoever left it here was here I'd tell him something he wouldn't forget soon. Not by a damn sight!"

But Ben could not move the car. It creaked and groaned when he pushed and when he pulled, but it would not budge a single inch. Knocking out his pipe and wiping his face, Ben led the team around the automobile through the undergrowth. When he got back into the lane he stopped the horses and went back to the car. He glanced inside for the first time.

"By Jesus!" Ben exclaimed highpitched.

Hastily glancing up the lane and down, he opened the door and pulled out a pair of silk stockings.

Ben was too excited to say anything, or to do anything. Still fingering the stockings he presently looked in the driver's seat, and there, to his surprise, under the steering-wheel sat a gallon jug of cider almost empty. Ben immediately pulled the cork to smell if it was hard. It was. He jabbed his thumb through the handle-hole and threw the jug in his elbow. It was hard all right, but there was very little of it left.

"Cromwell," he announced, smacking his lips with satisfaction, "that's pretty good cider, for a windfall."

As he carefully replaced the jug under the steering-wheel, Ben saw a garment lying on the floor. It was entangled with the do-funnys that operated the car. Carefully he pulled the garment out and held it before his eyes. He could not figure out just what it was, yet he knew it was something women wore pretty close to them. It was pinkish and it was silkish and it looked pretty. And there was very little of it. Ben stared open-mouthed and wild-eyed.

"By Jesus, Cromwell," Ben licked his mustache lip, "what do you know about that!"

Cromwell and the mare nibbled at the roadgrass, unconcerned.

Ben fingered the drawers a little more intimately. He turned them slowly around. Then he looked inside. Then he smelled them.

"It's a female thing, all right, Cromwell," Ben danced excitedly. "It's a female thing, all right!"

Holding the garment high in his hands, Ben climbed on the hayrack and drove down the lane into the highroad. The garment was nice and soft in his hands, and it smelled good, too.

He rode down the road thinking about the drawers. They filled him with the urge to do something out of the ordinary but he didn't know what he could do. When he reached Fred Williams' place he drew up the team. Fred's wife was stooping over in the garden. Ben pushed the garment carefully into his pants pocket.

"Nice day, to-day, Mrs. Williams," he called airily, his voice breaking foolishly. "Where's Fred?"

"Fred's gone to the village," she answered, looking around bent over her knees.

Ben's hand stole into the pocket feeling the garment. Even in his pocket out of sight it made him feel different to-day.

Hitching the team to the horserack, Ben went into the garden with Fred's wife. She was picking peas for supper. She wasn't bad-looking. Not by a damn sight!

Watching her while she pulled the peas from the vines, Ben strode around her in a circle, putting his hand into the pocket where the pink drawers were. Walking around her feeling the drawers, he had to spit every step or two. His mouth filled with water as fast as he could spit it out. The woman did not say much, and Ben said nothing at all. He was getting so now he could feel the drawers without even touching them with his hands.

Suddenly Ben threw his arms around her waist and squeezed her excitedly.

"Help!" she yelled at the top of her voice, diving forward. "Help!" she cried. "Help!"

When she dived forward both of them fell on the pea-vines tearing them and uprooting them. She yelled and scratched but Ben was determined and he held her with all his strength. They rolled in the dirt and on the pea-vines. Ben jerked out the pink drawers. They rolled over and over tearing up more of the pea-vines. Ben struggled to pull the drawers over her feet. He got one foot through one drawers-leg. They rolled down to the end of the row tearing up all the pea-vines. Fred would raise hell about his pea-vines when he came home!

Ben was panting and blowing like a horse at a horse-pulling but he could not get the other drawers-leg over the other foot. They rolled up against the fence and Fred's wife stopped struggling. She sat up looking down at Ben in the dirt. Both of them were brown with the garden soil, and Ben was sweating through his mask.

"Ben Hackett, what are you trying to do?" she sputtered through the earth on her face.

Ben released her legs and looked up at her. He did not say anything. She stood up, putting her foot in the empty leg, pulling the drawers up under her skirt. That was where he had been trying all this time to put them. Damn it!

Ben got up dusting his clothes. He followed her across the garden into the front yard.

"Wait here," she told him.

When she returned she carried a basin of water and a towel.

"Wash the dirt off your face and hands, Ben Hackett," she directed, standing over him, wearing the pink drawers.

Ben did as he was told to do. When he finished washing his face and hands he slapped some of the dirt out of his pants.

"It was mighty nice of you to bring the towel and water," he thanked her.

"You are halfway fit to go home now," she approved, pinning up her hair.

"Good-day," Ben said.

"Good-day," said Fred's wife.

ABOUT THE
EDITORS

MARTIN H. GREENBERG and **CHARLES G. WAUGH** are the country's most prolific anthologists. The former teaches political science at the University of Wisconsin at Green Bay. The latter teaches speech and psychology at the University of Maine at Augusta.